Diary of
HAKIM JONES
TRIALS, TRIBULATIONS, AND TRIUMPHS

JOE MASSENBURG JR.

Joseph Massenburg Publications
Email: joe.massenburg@gmail.com
Phone: +19732028051

ISBN: 979-8-89175-110-1 (sc)
ISBN: 979-8-89175-111-8 (ebk)

12 March 2014

M Y EARLIEST CHILDHOOD MEMORIES ARE WHEN I was no more than two or three; I stayed with my beloved grandmother in the projects on Lincoln Street because my parents worked full time. I was the apple of my grandmother's eye. My earliest memories of her are of a very caring and loving woman; I remember lying next to her and rubbing her braided hair. Even though I was only three when she passed, losing her still weighs greatly on my heart.

Grandmother kept me during the week, when my parents worked, and they took me on the weekends. After she died, I lived full time with my parents on 685 MLK Boulevard, a few blocks from Lincoln Street in the Central Ward in Newark, New Jersey. At the time, this brick tower building was a luxury high-rise apartment complex with doormen, elevator operators, and a beautiful court-yard. The first few years there were lovely. But then came the Section Eight and low-income-housing niggas, and the once-clean staircases and hallways became filthy with urine and shit from both humans and dogs. Most importantly, the crime rate in that neighborhood went up drastically.

One of my earliest memories is of Greg Austin, a young man who took a liking to my parents and me. Greg was sixteen years old; he often gave me his old toys and told people in the neighborhood that I was his little brother. One day when I was in kindergarten, I came home from school, and my mother told me that Greg had been shot and killed. That was the first time I thought about becoming a police officer. I wanted to catch whoever killed Greg and bring them to justice.

Growing up as an only child in that area was rough. I was often picked on and frequently got into fights with the other kids. I was often at a disadvantage because I didn't have any brothers or sisters to defend me. My one saving grace was my best friend, Marcus Peterson, who I met at Saint Mary's Elementary School. Marcus lived across the street in High Park Gardens and was an only child like me. Whenever I had trouble, he had my back. But growing up in the heart of the Central Ward was always an adventure. You had to watch your back 24/7 from stickup boys trying to rob you coming home from school or walking to the local supermarket. I saw so many people getting shot or thrown out of windows. I hated to even go outside. Stealing cars became prevalent then too. It was almost like a way of life.

My parents were very protective of me, especially my mother. My father made good money at the time. He worked at Pabst Blue Ribbon and could have moved us out of the hood. But he, like a lot of black men at that time, wanted to be a star in the hood. He always had to have a new Cadillac every few years, dress nice, and be ghetto fabulous. You still see the trend among a lot of brothers today. Black men, wake up! Providing a safe, stable environment for your family is more important than fancy cars and clothes. But as I think back, my father grew up in North Carolina, the son of a sharecropper. I guess when you grow up under such poor conditions, you are more inclined to think selfishly and not see the bigger picture.

As I got older, though, I saw my father for who he truly was: a selfish, controlling man who was inwardly miserable over his failures in life. That's why I now tell people that the negative forces that surround you bring negativity to you, even your own family, and, yes, I mean your mama, daddy, brothers, or sisters. Whoever carries a negative vibe, keep your distance from them. The universe is made up of energy. Negative energy breeds negative results. Every wonder why it seems as though no matter what you do, you can never get ahead? Think about it.

My father often claimed to be religious, but basically he became religious when it was beneficial for him. My mother was an old-fashioned woman with good morals who, like my grandmother, believed in family and standing by her man. Lord knows I don't know why she stood by my father for so many years. At times, he was both verbally and physically abusive to her. I often hated him, and to this very day, I could piss on his grave. I pray that almighty God Allah will have mercy on me, forgive me, and one day take that from my heart. Food for thought to the ladies and men out there: I know you get married for better or worse, but after a certain period of time, if it is not working, get out of it. You owe it to yourself to be happy.

During my early teen years, I began to train in boxing. I was never allowed to go outside much during the school year, so the only time I played sports was in school or during the summer. But at the request of my uncle Rosco, my parents allowed me to go to a little hole-in-the-wall boxing gym on South Eighth Street called Edmonds Gym. My parents didn't allow me to train every day though. I could only go on Friday and Saturday during the school year, but I was allowed to training regularly in the summer. Boxing was my outlet for all that life had put on me. Through boxing, I found a release for my inner demons, especially from an event that took place a year or so before I started training.

When I was eleven, two older guys walked past the playground of my grammar school and saw my friends and me playing football. I was always big for my size and usually did well at football when I got the chance to play and put my mind to it. They called me over to the fence and told me they had played football in school; they liked the way I played and said they would like to coach me. They told me to meet them after school, and we would go to a little park located near my house called Green Acres.

After school, I met up with them. They told me to first come with them to their house to get some equipment. Naïvely, I followed them. They took me to the second floor of the Prince Street projects, but when I saw the apartment was abandoned, I immediately knew something was wrong. I tried to leave, but they stopped me and tried to take off my clothes and have their way with me. I fought as hard as I could with everything I had in me. I kicked, punched, bit, and screamed at the top of my lungs until finally some people heard my screams and began knocking on the door. Some men then forced the door open and confronted my two assailants, giving me the opportunity to run downstairs and out of the building. I ran all the way home.

But after I made it home, I didn't tell my parents what had happened because I was afraid of how my father would react. I was never able to talk to him, and I believe this was one of the biggest factors in our strained relationship. People, please keep the lines of communication open with your children. Yes, they should always know that you are the parent, but they must feel comfortable enough to talk to you about anything, so don't alienate them.

Through boxing, I found confidence and courage to fight whatever challenges might arise. In the boxing ring, I often visualized that I was fighting my father or those two niggas who tried to assault me.

My high school years were trying times as well. I was seen as a geek at first, but luckily, I went to Bloomfield Tech, the same school as my cousin Anthony, who often looked out for me. As years went by, I met some good dudes who helped me through that geek phase. I also met some guys who, even though they later became gangsters, always had my back. One in particular was William Martin, who would years later be featured on the TV series Gangland as Doc Martin. He worked for the organized black mob in Atlanta. I often watched him and liked the confident way he carried himself. He was everything I wanted to be: tough, respected, and articulate.

In my later years in high school, I began to hang with the thugs, or the cool crowd, as they say. I sold loose joints (already-rolled weed) during and after school. I had to make it quick because my parents were always on me, but by then, I knew little ways to get around them, like telling them I needed to go to the library to study for a school assignment. During this time, I never had a girlfriend. I was never really allowed to be a kid and go through what most kids do.

Upon graduating from high school, I thought to myself, *I'm straight now. I'm eighteen and will get a good job and my own place and pursue boxing and do what I want.* Was I in for a rude awaking. My home life had become bad at the time because my father lost his job at Pabst. He was heavily in debt; the job he found paid nowhere near what he made before. He was not a well-educated man, so he did what he had to do; he was often even harsher to my mother during that period. I found it hard to get a job after high school and when I finally did get a job, it only paid four dollars an hour. My mother was forced to go back to work. My father was the one who initially asked her not to work after my grandmother died so that she could devote her time to taking care of me.

My first job as an adult was at Regency Motors, a car dealer in Montclair, New Jersey. I liked the job because they sold Jaguars, Rolls-Royces, and Volvos and I liked working around the nice cars.

Around the time of my nineteenth birthday, I officially converted to Islam, which changed my life in the most profound way. I became much more comfortable in my own skin. I found peace within myself, I finally developed a relationship with my Lord. Growing up an only child, I always felt alone. In Islam, I now had a worldwide brotherhood under one god, Allah. I often conflicted with my father, who was supposed to be a Christian, but to me he will forever be a hypocrite; he often called the white man the devil, but it's been my experience in life that most of the devils here on earth have usually been the same color as me. Religion, I believe, is used by people in general to control other people, to keep them passive and believing that no matter how bad a person is to you here on earth, God will make it better in the next life. Whites used that on us in slavery, and blacks have also tried to use religion to justify their corruptions.

Islam is a way of life, a way of living in a righteous and respectful manner. Some religions put more emphasis on what awaits you after you die. Now there are some Muslims who just get into the spiritual aspect of Islam, but my understanding of Islam deals with the spiritual, mental, and physical. Now don't get me wrong; I believe in the hereafter and that the next life is the one that really matters, but I also believe as wise men like the honorable Elijah Muhammad said, why is it we as a people always feel we have to die to experience heaven? Allah tells us in the Koran to get the good in this world and the best in the hereafter. Most of these pastors, preachers, and naysayers tell you about the next life, but you ever look at how they're living? I just say, let's keep it real. Islam also encouraged me to seek knowledge and understanding of the world going on around me.

At age twenty, I enrolled at Essex County College as a criminal justice major. I loved the whole college atmosphere; it felt so good to be around the positive vibes of educated people, who were attempting to do something for themselves and not relying on someone to do something for them. My economic situation continued to stop me from enjoying the full benefits of this life. I still lived at home because I could not afford an apartment of my own. I had to pay rent at my house; even though I only made peanuts at work, I had to pay half the rent at home, and on top of that, I had to pay for college credits because they had some clause at school if you were under twenty-four, it was assumed you still lived at home, which I did, but little did they know I had to pay half the rent. So you can only imagine how broke I was. Women were often attracted to me, but I was broke, so it was far in between when I had a girlfriend.

During those hard times, only Islam and Allah the almighty kept me intake. I soon became frustrated with life. My neighborhood around me did not help either; the crack really made things bad. I remember seeing the crack lines stretching all the way around the block. I saw drug boys with nice cars, money, and women. I was busting my ass doing the right thing, with no results. I soon met some radicals Muslims who followed a different doctrine, the new world nation of Islam. I didn't agree with their interpretation of the faith, but I supported their belief; why should we suffer while the unrighteous succeed?

I soon got together with some of the brothers, and we made plans to rob drug dealers in New York. I saved what little money I could and purchased a 38 special. I went on several journeys to various locations in New York with them; we would watch, wait, and then move in when the time was right. During this period of my life, I became cold and mean. I often thought about killing my father, catching him alone in the apartment when my mother was at work or finding him lying down in bed and blowing his head off; the only thing that stopped me most days was the thought of my mother coming to visit me in jail for killing my own father. It would kill her.

I liked the money I was getting for the robberies. One time, after we forced our way into a dealer's apartment, I saw one of guys

I was running with put a gun to a baby's head and make the dealer tell where the drug stash was. I saw myself beginning to change as a person. I was become more cold hearted and vicious. Until this time, I managed to avoid going to jail or being arrested, but I realized if I continued down this path I would probably end up in jail or dead.

It was during this time my life took a sudden turn for the best, after I was laid off from my job at the car dealer. I considered becoming a drug dealer myself, but a gift came for me in the mail one Saturday morning: I got the results from the law enforcement test I had taken a few months earlier. I passed the test with a score of 90. After getting my score, there was hope; a few months after that, I passed my background check, passed the physical, and soon was scheduled to go into the academy. It seemed as if the creator himself saw me going in a direction that I shouldn't be going, and he gave me a shot at another direction, a better direction.

After finishing the academy and becoming a police officer, I never again thought about a life of crime; my friends or associates (whatever you want to call them) were shocked to see me as an officer. But in spite of being shocked and surprised, they seemed to be sincerely happy for me. Many of them said they were proud of me and they wished they hadn't messed their records up so they could become cops. My earlier years on the job were a little rough until I got a feel for the work, but it was worth it to change my life for the better in every way.

I now had economic security. I stayed at home to look out for my mother; mainly, my father now sensed that if he ever became abusive, I would either lock him up or kill him. My situation with the ladies greatly improved. Since becoming a cop, I've had more than my share of women. See what driving a nice car will do for you? I was in relationships with some of them; many were just sexual. I blew more than my share of money in go-go bars as well. This is something that a lot of young men from the hood get caught up in; they were taught the more women you fucked, the more of a man you were. I'm here to tell you that a man cannot really become his highest unless he can control his lower desires. They say it ain't trickin' if you got it; I say if you wanna keep it, stop tricking. And remember, fellas: no matter how you make your money, you can't focus 100 percent on the paper if you're chasing women. When they get mad at you, they will be the first ones to turn state on you.

On the subject of relationships, as I stated earlier, I have had many; some of them stand out, though, like my friend Sasha. She was a real freak; I mean she sucked dick, licked balls, and took it in the ass. She liked to get it in every hole you can think of; she was also a good-hearted person, but she had a drug problem. She stayed in and out of jail, so you know I couldn't go beyond sex with her. I'll tell you, women are very complicated; Sasha eventually ended up having a baby with another crack head, and they moved down to North Carolina together. I wish her the best.

I loved the go-go bars; I used to frequent all the local ones: Benny's Doll House, Slicks, World Paradise. I knew them all. It was difficult finding a good woman, even in the mosques; most black sisters from this area love thugs. A lot of the women of faith seemed more interested in niggas in jail. I really believe black women subconsciously enjoy being treated bad.

Another young lady who stood out to me is my friend Temicka; when I met her, she said she was gay (something that's big amongst young women in urban hoods these days, and I don't knock it). I have gay family members, and I love them no less. But this girl Temicka goes with a chick who looks like a man, dresses like man, and acts like a man. With all this said, she might as well go with a man. Temicka used to always come to me when this gorilla dike started to mistreat her, but I had to put an end to that; the pussy was good when I got it, but it was not worth the headaches.

My love life stayed the same until I turned thirty-two. I met a beautiful young lady in a go-go bar, of all places. Her dancer name was Sexual Chocolate; as soon as we met, I knew she was the one, even though she danced. I had never connected with a sister like I connected with her. We hit it off in every way, both mentally and spiritually. By that, I mean it wasn't just about sex with her; we would often have deep conversations on many subjects. She explained that she only danced while she was attending Bronx Community College; she wanted to stop dancing once she finished school. After a couple of years dating, I knew she was the woman I wanted to marry, but there was just my little home situation.

By now, my parents and I had purchased a home together, and I didn't want to leave them out there. So I had some serious thinking to do. How could I afford to take care of them and take care of my own family? A short time later, my father became ill; he went to the doctor and was diagnosed with stage-four stomach cancer. He fought a brave battle but passed a year later. My mother took his passing hard, even after everything they had been together over forty years. After his passing, my lady Jennifer moved in with me and my mom, and we were married later on the same year. By now I was the head of the house (hell, even when my father was alive, I paid the mortgage).

Throughout my adult life, I continued my education; I always took a class here and there. Within two years, I earned my degree in journalism; writing had always been a passion of mine. I finished my career as a police officer at age forty-seven; Jennifer stopped dancing after we got married. She finished school and worked as a nursing supervisor at the University of Medicine and Dentistry of New Jersey (UMDNJ). After retiring, I was blessed enough to get an entry-level position as an investigative reporter for CNN. My life these days has really taken off. I loved being a police officer, but a journalist is who I was always meant to be. My job title involves uncovering corruption; I enjoy discovering hidden facts and bringing them to the public. I have been blessed to write two books that became best sellers. The second half of my life has brought me many blessings, especially financially. I sold the house in Newark and now live in a huge house in Upper Montclair. Of course, Mom is with us; as long as the good Lord blesses me to have her with me, I will take care of her.

My life as a journalist has taken me places I never thought I would ever go; it now seems like it was another lifetime ago when I was a kid living in Brick Towers. I reflect back on some of the people I knew growing up there. In the hood, you meet some real characters; you meet your share of killers, thugs, and criminals, but you also meet some of the best people in the world. When I was younger and first became a cop, I wanted to clean up the hood. I thought the worst criminals were in the hoods, but after being involved in the system for as long as I was a police officer, I'd say that the true criminals go much further than the urban ghettos. Heavy crime becomes an issue because of social and economic factors. Having a good educational system, a good and steady economic state, and a good social environment are essential to the proper growth and development of any society.

Being an investigative reporter has really opened my eyes as to who the real predators are in this world. Some of these corrupt politicians and legislators continue to fatten their own pockets and could care less about pushing for legislation to improve our inner cities. For certain people, crime in the inner city is a profitable business. Some of these CEO of major insurance firms are making a killing off of insurance policies in the hood. So put two and two together and think about it: If crime is profitable to certain people, then imagine what they would be willing to pay someone to vote against legislation that could help make crime lower. That's why I love doing my job, whenever I'm able to draw attention to this corruption. Now, I'm able to speak out about it, and I'm able to help out financially in the hood. With the help of my wife, I have started a nonprofit organization that counsels troubled youths and women who have been the victim of sexual assault. Wow, life is something; to think I used to rob drug dealer. It just goes to show how your life can turn around 180 degrees. Allah is great.

My new life as a reporter has made me a lot of enemies. Exposing people has a way of doing that. But that's cool; after growing up in the Central Ward, whatever life sends at me from this point on is a piece of cake. As a police officer, I was involved in two shootings; I've been injured several times in the line of duty. All in all, I must say in spite of the ups and downs, if I had to do it again, I wouldn't change a thing. As a reporter, I have had my life threatened on several occasions. I have been sued three times, and I'm pretty sure there are a number of politicians who would love to have me silenced, one way or another.

13-Mar-2014

I MADE A VOW TO CONTINUE MY FIGHT for justice, by fighting with the pen. At one time, I thought the best solution to problems was the fist and a gun. Now that I have evolved, I've learned through life's experiences that the pen is much mightier than the sword. If you want to make it count, put it on paper. Violence will only lead to more violence. With the pen, you will get redemption. The best battles are won and lost on paper.

This book belongs exclusively to the owner: Joseph Massenburg Jr.

14-Mar-2014

This book is a tale of redemption; it is the fictional story of a young man growing up in the bowels of Newark, New Jersey, one of the toughest inner cities in the country. It is an uplifting story of a young man who overcomes many hardships and circumstance to turn his life around and succeed, in spite of these challenges. The book addresses some of the many problems that inner city youths deal with regularly. Young black men in particular have dealt with subjects like education, financial independence, sexuality, and family. This book is meant to be uplifting and to show that with faith in the Lord above and with plenty of hard work, difficulties and hardship can be overcome. I hope to do inspire dreams. Remember, it is important to persevere in life with patience; life is a marathon, not a sprint. Things don't always happen right away, but with dedication, hard work, and determination, goals can and will be met. So sit back, relax, and enjoy his life, my story, my book. Redemption is only a step away.

15-Mar-2014

Growing up in the Central Ward was an adventure. It had its moments; you never knew what to expect. Behind every corner, there was usually something or someone lurking around begging for a handout, trying to run a hustle, or looking to do a stickup. Drug dealing was the major economic resource, followed by other hustles to make some money, like running numbers, prostitution, and stealing cars. When I was small, I went to Saint Mary's Elementary School; my parents, like a lot of black parents, believed there was no better education than going to a Catholic school. At that time, you didn't hear anything about priest molesting little boys or anything like that.

I was a pretty good student, especially my first six years. I stayed on the honor roll, but around seventh grade, that all changed. I still passed all of my classes, but it seemed like no matter what I did, I could not make the honor roll again. My problem was giving in to peer pressure in the hood; getting good grades and being smart wasn't cool. It's disturbing, now that I think about it: Niggas honestly used to brag about failing classes and going to summer school. I'm glad I never had to deal with that. I wanted my summers to myself.

Those nuns at the Catholic school were like prison guards. When I was around twelve, I could feel myself starting to rebel. It felt like I was in jail, at school and at home. I began to feel as though I had the weight of the world on my shoulders; after everything I had been though, after what had happened to me in the projects, I began to hate my life and almost everything in it. Life in the Central Ward wasn't all bad; I have more than my share of fond memories, but the bad ones were life altering. But that was life in the hood; it was either feast or famine, as far as emotions went. You were either very happy or sad and mad as hell.

My adolescent years were turbulent; going to school could be an adventure in itself. I often felt like vultures and predators were just lying in wait for me to come by. As I stated before, being an only child in the hood was hard. My father was an odd man who didn't like to associate with many people. He wasn't even close to his own family. It seemed like everybody in the hood had backup, everybody but me. I had a few friends in the neighborhood, but it was only a very select few who I could say had my back no matter what. Even with the odds against me, I still had to fight because in these streets, if you don't fight, you're only gonna make your situation even harder. Poverty had a way of making people feel angry all of the time; at times, my rage almost consumed me. I often thought, *If only I could kill one of these pieces of shit and get away with it.*

Tragedy was a way of life growing up. I remember a young lady named Valery who lived in my building. She was several years older than me; she was a pretty young lady a good student and very nice person. One day, she was killed at the bodega across the street from my building, shot in the head by some punk ass son of a bitch who was robbing the store. I mean, damn, he couldn't just get the money and keep it moving; he had to kill such a bright attractive girl with a good future ahead of her.

Even paying your respects at a wake or funeral was dangerous. I'll never forget being at Perry's Funeral Home one evening with my family, paying our respects to a friend of the family. In the next room, Malik, a drug dealer from the neighborhood, was being viewed by family and friends when out of nowhere, a group of Africans who Malik had been beefing with ran into the room, shot up the body, and turned over the casket. Incidents like this further inspired me to become a police officer. Stolen cars were like a way of life; you heard cars squeaking all day and night, kids stealing cars and doing dough-nuts were the norm. I once saw a stolen car spin out of control and run a young lady over; all you saw was her brains bleeding all over the sidewalk.

I don't really know why it took me so long to lose my virginity; in the hood, you had sisters selling their bodies all of the time just to get high. During the crack decades, you could get sucked off for as little as three dollars. In the late eighties, early nineties, I did notice a slight change in the hood; people became more conscious of their culture. I saw a large number of people convert to Islam, as I myself did at seventeen, first with the Nation of Islam (NOI) and then as a Muslim who follows the sunna of Prophet Muhammad, may Allah be pleased with him.

I also saw many brothers and sisters get into Afrocentrism; also the 5 percent teachings were big in most urban hoods. This cultural movement did help to bring a certain sense of togetherness in the hood, but at the end of the day, certain old habits are hard to break. Around the middle nineties, a few years after I became a police officer, I saw a gang culture start developing in the hood. I mean, growing up, there were always gangs out: the Wild Bunch, the Lollipops, the Avenues. But now we had Bloods and Crips, just like the West Coast. You had brothers killing each other and going toward other colors. You saw cats who were best friends growing up and even family members going to war with each other over colors. As a policeman, I had many dealings with gang members; I often had to arrest them, and there were confrontations with some of them, but over time, a lot of brothers gained mad respect for me.

I would sit down and talk to some of them; I began to see what I probably already knew, that many of them grew up in similar circumstances like mine. I saw that a lot of them were not totally bad kids, just products of a vicious cycle of ignorance that continues to trouble urban hoods to this very day. The father figure is vital in the upbringing of a male child. I had my father in my home growing up, but I will tell you from first-hand experience, even if the father is in the house, if he ain't shit, him being in the house is irrelevant. A father has to be a living, breathing role model for a child. Most old heads think that feeding and clothing a child makes you a great father, but what about spending time with that child, encouraging him to dream and to reach for his goals?

I believe a lot of old heads are often jealous of younger people; a lot of them never really accomplished shit in their life, so they really don't wanna see their sons go somewhere, but that's just my opinion. A lot of the blame goes to our black women and the decisions they make and the fucked-up niggas they have kids with. My mother, unfortunately, married an ignorant-ass country nigga from North Carolina; as I stated before, I see a lot of sisters dealing with dudes who aren't worth a good shit. These lowlifes abuse and treat them like shit, but they still stand by them. It makes me think back to that book this sister wrote in the 1990s: *The Black Man's Guide to Understanding the Black Woman;* sisters were up in an outrage about that book, but maybe that sister was right. Some women need to be dogged in order for them to act right. I hope I'm wrong, but from my own experience, every time I start off a relationship being loving and kind, the woman tried to shine on me and take advantage of me, but once I put my foot down and showed them the thug in me, it was all good. A lot of sisters also like a man who is passive and who they can control. Black women in general call the shots, especially if she is a sister with a halfway good job making a few dollars; you can't tell her anything. It's hard to meet a balanced young lady; the way things are these days, it's either of the two extremes: They want an abusive man or a cream puff, not a well-balanced gentleman.

16-Mar-2014

THE IMPORTANCE OF EDUCATION WAS ALWAYS STRESSED to me by my mother, and I love her for it. The education system has failed many of us in the inner cities. Most inner city schools are way behind the schools in the suburbs. I feel a lot of that comes from the parents. Parents in the hood must get more involved in their children's education. I first saw examples of this when I went to St. Mary's; there were many parents who just dropped their kids off to school and left everything up to the teachers. I remember a kid who came up with me from first grade until eighth grade, a kid named Ronald Austin. He stands out to a degree because he was the only white boy in my class; his mom worked during the day but was a prostitute by night; not by choice but because she had to. His father had left with her with five children, and let's keep it real: She needed the income. But unfortunately, due to her very complex schedule, she was unable to spend time with him to help him with his studies. Ron often struggled in school, and you could see other kids whose parents didn't put in the effort, how different their grades were compared to kids whose parents were active in the school and constantly inquiring about their child's education.

When we were in fifth grade, Ron's mother passed away from the AIDS virus; back then, nobody knew much about this illness. Several years later, the whole world would know of that dreaded disease. Ronald did manage to graduate grammar school, and that was pretty much the last time I saw him. I heard years later that he dropped out of high school and moved to Florida. The last thing I heard, he was serving time down there on a homicide charge; as I reflect back on him, it just goes to show whether your black or white, if you grow up in a violent area with little education, no family structure, and a poor economy, it's a lot tougher trying to succeed in this world (not impossible, but certainly tougher).

I always found time to continue school in some way. Every little bit helps with education; not only does it help open doors for you in the professional world, it opens your mind. Growing up surrounded by projects can have a detrimental effect on a person; I know it did on me, but by reading and studying, my mind was able to escape the hood mentality. I was able to focus on escaping my gloomy surroundings and circumstances. As a police officer, I worked out of different commands during my career. I started in the East Precinct and stayed most of my career there, and then I went to traffic for a few years and finished my career in community affairs. I enjoyed every command, but I especially loved community affairs because for most of my tenure, I enforced the law (which was what I signed up for). In community affairs, I was able to really interact with different members of the city, and in working in this capacity, I did more than just arrest people; I was able to counsel people and get to know more of their inner feelings. I got to show people the more human side of policing. Don't get me wrong, policing in Newark is a tough job, and the men and women of this department do an awesome job. I'm just saying as officers, we are often caught up in just making arrests and enforcing the law, which is essential and much needed in the inner cities, but we can sometimes lose focus on another very important job description we have. How about helping people and saving lives? By saving lives, I'm not just talking about the physical act. I'm talking about giving good sound advice and piloting them in the right direction. I liked community affairs because while taking them to jail is a necessary evil, in community affairs, I was able to influence them and lead them in another direction other than jail.

17-Mar-2014

JUST STARTING TO GET TO KNOW MY family. Over the past five years since my father died, I've really started to get to know my family on my father's side. Growing up, I was extremely close to my mother's side of the family, and I've noticed during my life that a lot of kids who grow up in black communities shared the same fate, especially black males; for some reason, you're just not close to your father's side. I rarely saw my aunts and cousins on Dad's side of the family. He visited his family, but he rarely took me with him. I used to wonder what was up; was he ashamed of me? As I've gotten older, I realize the importance of family. My mother's immediate family is not very large, and over the years, almost all of my aunts uncles and cousins have passed. After a while, you start to think you are alone in the world. But Allah is good, and he will never forsake you; where that side may be small, my father's side seems almost endless, and even though I'm just getting to know them, I feel very close to the ones I've met. I just wish I had met them earlier.

As a police officer, it is sometimes hard to trust people; establishing friendships can be difficult, so often it is easy for me to hang with my family. I generally feel more comfortable with those I share blood ties with. My next mission as far as it relates to family is to start my own family. I can't wait to start having kids with my baby, Jennifer, the love of my life. I want very much to have a son; now, don't get me wrong: I would love a daughter with all my heart, but I'm hoping for a chance do everything with my son that my father never did with me. I look forward to being an example to him of what a man should be and show how a real man should present himself. But let me make it perfectly clear: No matter what my child's gender is, I will love and support him or her in all matters. I don't care if I look like a bum, as long as my kids look good and are well taken care of.

On May 13, 2013, Jennifer made me the happiest man on the planet when she informed me that she was pregnant with our child; finally, at forty-four, I was going to be a father. I used to think it was never going to happen, but Allah is great. Then on February 5, 2014, my little son Amir Jones was born; the birth brought about a change in me in every way. At one time, an inner rage and anger fueled my passions, even though I was successful in life. Due to my turbulent upbringing, I always carried a chip on my on my shoulder, and I've always hated my father. Now as a father myself, the rage inside of me began to subside. I slowly began to forgive my father for whatever wrongs he did to me. I knew from this point on, I had to be a living example of positive conduct for a little one of my own, and to walk around carrying hatred in my heart was not good for me or my child. I may not have grown up in the nicest of areas, but because of the mercy of the Almighty, I could now give my family a better environment to live in. With hard work and undying faith in God, we can redeem our past with a better future. The key is you must believe and never surrender to the devil. Don't let anger and self-pity consume you; if one thing doesn't work, try something else.

18-Mar-2014

ONE OF MY MOST CHALLENGING ASSIGNMENTS AS an investigative reporter was on the subject of racism in America: fact or a matter of perception? This subject is a very touchy topic with many people; you often hear many people, especially those in the inner cities, blaming the system for not getting ahead. Many believe, as my father believed, that the white man is holding them back. For my investigation, I spoke to a number of people of different races and got many different views on the subject. From there, I looked at statistics showing the differences between how much money each race makes on average, the educational gap between each race, and life expectancy between each race. And while I must say the advantages clearly go to the white race, I believe that as human beings, we can to a large extent control our own destiny. I am living proof how a person's life can change.

I'm not saying that racism is not alive and well in America. I am saying that in spite of everything, this country, the United States of America, is the greatest nation in the world and gives all of us a chance to change our situations. You have to look into your own soul and see what is holding you back from living up to your own potential. In most cases, it is you or one of your own. You can't get mad at others for sticking together, as they were raised to do. When you get people united and standing together for a common cause, you will get good results. If you spend your time criticizing each other and stabbing each other in the back, then guess what? Your results are usually negative. I think back to when I first became a police officer; many people in my family tried to talk me out of it, people like my father, who didn't want to see me become economically independent.

His philosophy was, whoever makes the most money in the house controls the house. How in the hell can you call the white man an oppressor when you are an oppressor yourself? I learned that you can't look to another race to help improve your condition; you have to make strides to become independent in every way, economically and socially. In order to do that, you must be patient; nothing good happens overnight. You must be willing to crawl first and then gradually start to take steps, and before long, you will not only walk but you will be off and running. I think back to when I was washing cars and cleaning toilets at the car dealer. I wondered if I would ever get ahead. Now look at me.

19-Mar-2014

Growing up in the Central Ward, you learned how to handle problems and challenges in your own way; when I wasn't involved in a fight myself, I remember looking out of my eighth-floor window, which looked directly into the courtyard. I could usually count on seeing a good fight. Different families were always going at it, especially in the summer. It was like being at the Friday night fights every night. At least during this period, fights were just that: a good fistfight. Don't get me wrong, you still had your fair share of people who got shot, but back then, it was mainly just the people who were in the game who got shot. Nowadays, the first thing these cats do is get the guns, and innocent bystanders often get hit in the cross fire. Back then, if someone had a beef with you, they settled it with you, not your mother, not your kids, not your girl. Matters that need to be settled were still settled in the hood, no matter what era or generation.

Being an only child and without knowing just how big my family was, I often had to pick and choose my battles carefully. I mean, I couldn't go up against a family too big. Then again, certain violations you just can't let go, like the time those two older guys tried to sexually assault me. I never forgot the wrong that they attempted on me. I never spoke of it to my parents; certain things you didn't report to the police, you just kept it under wraps until the right time came to even the score. During that somewhat troubled period of my life, when I was involved with those brothers from that more radical sect of Islam, I came across those two young men. I rarely saw them after the initial incident, usually from a distance, but I always thought to myself, *One day, I will even the score.* That time came almost ten years later when I saw that they had moved in on Hunterdon Street.

I explained what had taken place several years earlier to the brothers, and they were all in. They said, "Let's make it right." So we began watching out for them, watching when they came in and what time they usually made certain moves. From all that I saw, it appeared as though they were now just working men getting on with their lives, but I'm from the block. I don't forgive or forget. One night, me and four of the brothers found out where they lived. One of the brothers was proficient at picking locks; he got us into the apartment. We locked the doors and waited; when they came home that night, they came home to four guns on them. We made sure to cover ourselves with masks and gloves; we tied them up and gagged them and proceeded to beat them within an inch of their lives; when we finished, we had broken both of their arms and legs. We managed to leave without a clue. Their souls belonged to the Lord, but their black asses belonged to me.

20-Mar-2014

Power of Positive Thinking

GROWING UP IN A HARSH ENVIRONMENT AND under gloomy conditions can definitely affect one's thinking. Often in poor urban communities, you see a lot of negativity, even in the schools. I remember teachers who were quick to tell you, "No, that goal is not for you; you should try this instead." Granted, you should be practical in whatever decisions you make in life. But who has the right to tell you not to shoot for the stars in whatever you wish to do? If anything, give children a practical and positive blueprint toward achieving their goals.

As I child, I wanted to be a musician. I remember one of the assistant teachers in my first-grade class, Mrs. Langford, telling me that was a silly dream, that I should try for a better goal like being a doctor or lawyer. Those are wonderful careers, if that's what you want to do, but if that isn't were your heart is leading you, why should someone try to push this on you?

I first thought of being a police officer when I was in the sixth grade. I vividly remember my sixth-grade teacher, Mrs. Lawrence. I never quite knew how to take her. She was a very attractive woman with pretty brown skin, and she had some body. I mean breast and ass; for days during my puberty years, I had many wet dreams about her. In sixth grade, however, I had to be constantly on guard with her. I never knew what type of mood she would be in; some days, she was sweet and nice, but other days, she was like the bitch from hell. I guess maybe on those days she was on PMS. In the sixth grade, I first mentioned during a class project that I wanted to be a police officer. I guess maybe this was one of her PMS days, but she laughed and then said being a cop definitely wasn't for me; it didn't match my personality.

Wow, I think back about how wrong she was. I believe your dreams and goals are the way that your soul expresses to you who you truly are. That why I'll tell anyone, "Follow your dreams; even if it fails you, at least you followed your heart, and don't let anyone, no matter who it is, steal your dreams." Even at an early age, I saw a lot of older niggas were envious of the youth from the hood; if they didn't make it, they really didn't want you to make. I often hear older heads say how it was when they were coming up, how if you did wrong in their time, your neighbors would discipline you and then when you got home, your parents got with you. Okay, if that way was so damn good, then why didn't you raise your kids that way? I remember growing up in the bricks; if you looked at someone's child the wrong way, even when the child did wrong, you had an all out family brawl. If I had listened to these niggas growing up, I wouldn't be the man that I am today. People of substance grow and develop over the course of their life. I wonder how a person can make a judgment on someone like a child. Life has a way of changing people, either for the better or the worse. At twenty-three, you're not gonna be the same person you were when you were eleven. A few years into my career, I saw Mrs. Lawrence when I was patrolling the downtown area; we had a pleasant exchange. She seemed shocked to see me as a cop. I'll admit it: Even though she is sixteen years older than me (at the time when I saw her, I was twenty-eight), I would still like to hit it. That ass was still phat as hell (lol).

I can't put enough emphasis on the power of the human mind; that's why it is extremely important to think and behave in a positive manner in every aspect of your life. I have read many books on the subject of quantum physics, and I'm a true believer that as human beings, we have the power to will something to happen (of course, with the help of God and with work and dedication from you). I have seen from my own experiences when I went into a situation with self-doubt and just merely hoped for a good outcome, I usually would come up short. Now if I go into something with a positive outlook, I am not going to be denied; no matter what, I have had great success. That's why I distance myself from negative-thinking people.

One of the main reasons I was able to survive twenty-five years as a cop in the big city is because I don't keep many cop friends. Now, I'm not trying to dis my coworkers; I have met many good people on this job, but cops often have very pessimistic attitudes toward life; some guys are always looking at the bad side of everything and always expecting the worst. Hell, my own mother (and I love her with all my heart) always thinks about the bad before the good. Well, people are going to be who they are; I guess that's all they can be, but in order to move forward, a successful and positive attitude and mind-set is vital.

21-Mar-2014

S A YOUNG MAN, I BELIEVED THAT my masculinity, my manhood, was based on how many chicks I could bag and fuck. I guess a lot of this had to do with me losing my virginity late. My self-esteem suffered after all of the drama and craziness I endured growing up I was naturally a shy person; that, along with my hardships, caused me to have poor self-esteem. As a teenager, I had no game whatsoever. I was often very hesitant when approaching a girl. I would sometimes have to mentally talk myself into just trying to talk to a girl. I didn't break virginity until I was almost twenty-two. I'll never forget my first; she was an older woman named Gail. She was thirty at the time, a red bone with long dark hair, and thick as hell; she was very sensual and provocative. I used to see her when I'd walk home from Essex County College; we would always speak, and she often told me I had such pretty hazel eyes. I'm glad she approached me first because Lord knows I wasn't confident enough to approach her at the time.

After talking with her over a period of time, she invited me over to her house one night. The first time I came over, we just talked and got to know each other. She was very healing for me. I confided in her about a lot of my insecurities with women and my self-esteem issues. I lucked out meeting her; with the mentality of most hood hoes, they would love to meet a young naïve brother like me, so they could take advantage of me. But baby girl was so sweet and understanding. She had one of the sexiest and most seductive manner I have ever seen. On the second date over her crib, I came off; we started off kissing me. She then gave me the blowjob of a lifetime. Then came the main course: She put a condom on me and rode me like a wild stallion. I lost contact with her a few months later when she moved, and I've only seen her here and there over the years, but man, I thank her to this day for getting me over the hump.

After getting broke in, I was on the hunt, especially after becoming a cop. I wanted to nail every hole I could. I had threesomes with two women; I have sexed as many as four women in one day and then at night sexed my lady. I was on a rampage, I guess making up for lost time. I must say, though, I always practiced safe sex because in spite of my little sex addiction, I never wanted kids out of marriage because I always saw how child support used to break my friends' pockets.

Plus, most important these days is that I have gone forty-plus years disease free (not even crabs). Now as a married man, I think back, *Wow, if only I knew then what I know now; a real man is never defined by his achievements in bed but by success and achievements in life.* Achieving goals and overcoming adversity are things to be proud of; they are what you should leave behind as your legacy, not a bunch of children out of wedlock who you know you can't take care of. Now as a father, it is my responsibility to instill this in my son, to think more with the head on his neck and not the one between his legs.

I thank Allah for saving me from myself, especially when it came to women. I think back to a particular incident one evening at Benny's go-go bar; there was a dancer there named Passion. She was a sexy chocolate thing and had an ass like a government mule. I had seen her previously in the bar; she always came on to me, so one night after quite a bit of drinking I made arrangements to go to a hotel with her. I went over to the gas station across the street from the bar and picked up a package of condoms; of course, that's a must. I then proceeded to wait for her; several minutes went by, and she still hadn't left the club, so I waited a few more minutes and then I went back in to see what was up. She was still on stage, dancing. When I asked her what happened, she said she couldn't go that night because her boyfriend had just walked in. I never got to hit that, but God is so good: A few months later, I heard that she had the AIDS virus. Then two years later, Passion died from it. I think back now, what if I had fucked her? Even though I would have used a condom, what if it broke? And even if it didn't, I wouldn't have wanted that on my mind. Just goes to show that a night of freaky pleasure can lead to a lifetime of pain.

22-Mar-2014

HOBBIES AND RECREATIONAL ACTIVITIES HAVE ALSO PLAYED an important in helping me keep it all together over the years. After putting in eight hours (or more) a day as a cop in Newark, you need some healthy outlets to take your mind off the BS you see and everything you have to deal with out here. Bowling has been an off-and-on hobby of mine for years now. I never joined a bowling league or bowled in any tournaments, something I now regret because I think a competitive environment like that is always good for character. I would go bowling from time to time with a few friends, just for a recreational outlet. Boxing played a big part in my life when I was younger, and of course, I still trained into adulthood. As I got older, I started training young kids in the sport. Boxing has always been my passion, and through training these kids, I was able to continue my dream through them. I also try to counsel these young men and be a good role model to them.

There was one kid I'm especially proud of, a young man named Jeremy Brown. I first met him when he was seven years old; I was twenty-seven at the time. His grandmother brought him to Red Brick Gym for training to help toughen him up because he was being picked on at his grammar school. When I first started working with him, he was a skinny little kid; he couldn't do one push-up. The poor kid was shy and had already gone through a lot; his mother was a crack head, and his father was serving a long prison sentence. His grandmother was stuck taking care of him and his two sisters.

I took my time training Jeremy. I had to help him build not only his body but also his self-esteem. It took awhile, but his consistency and determination paid off; two years later, he was winning junior Olympic tournaments. I gave him up to another trainer a few years later because of my work schedule; I was unable to give him all of the time that he needed. He is twenty now, and after a stellar amateur career, he's ready to turn pro, and he recently graduated from Union County College. I am so proud of this young man.

Another hobby of mine, which I strayed away from for a number of years, is writing. By writing, I'm able to express myself and vent in a creative way. Writing was my way of escaping the reality of my troubled life when I was younger. It's not good to always vent in a physical way. That can get you into trouble. Venting on paper, however, is creative, and for me, it was just as good of an outlet for my feelings. I never knew how much writing would do for me in the near future.

23-Mar-2014

Ghetto Advice

THE BIGGEST DRAWBACKS IN MY LIFE HAVE happened when taking advice from nothing happening, no-account negroes from the hood. Hood niggas are always in your business, and they always want to put their two cents in and give you advice on a matter, even if they know nothing about it. If I had a nickel for all of the times one of these goons tried to advise me on a matter, I could have retired five years earlier. Especially some older heads, who love to give advice. Believe me, wisdom doesn't always come with age. Like I stated earlier, there are a lot of haters in the hood, a lot of jealousy, especially with older people; if they don't make it, they don't wanna see nobody make it. Before you take advice from someone, first take a look at the person giving you the advice; if they don't have anything to show in life and haven't accomplished a damn thing themselves, what the hell can they show you? All they can do is be an example of what not to do.

I remember as a young patrolman, I was very aggressive, making plenty of arrests and making a name for myself on the streets. There was a lieutenant on the job named John Haywood; he was feared on the streets of Newark. When he was younger, he was notorious for chasing down the bad guys; he was also known for taking no shit and kicking ass when he had to. Another thing he had a rep on the streets for was taking drug boys' money. He was one of my lieutenants earlier in my career; he always appeared to like me, but you know how you just get that feeling about someone. Whenever I would get a good arrest, he would find some fault with the job, even if another lieutenant had already signed off on the job. He would always say he was only trying to make me a better officer. I always knew what the real deal was: He hated to see a young nigga come along and get respect on the street similar to the respect he used to get.

One day, I caught a robbery suspect downtown who had punched a lady in the face and took two gold chains from her. I caught the kid a few blocks from where the incident took place. After finishing the paperwork at the precinct, I turned in two golds chains as evidence to Lieutenant Haywood, who was sitting behind the desk. A few weeks later, I got a call from the property room supervisor; the property sheet said two gold chains were submitted but there was only one chain in the property bag. When I confronted Lieutenant Haywood about it, he said only one chain was submitted; well, my question was if only one chain was submitted, why did he sign off on a sheet that said two chains were submitted? Then we I had to go before the trial board at police trials, he advised me to take a plea of three days' suspension because if I tried to fight it, they might really hammer me with suspension time. I listened to him then, but as I think back now, I say never give in; stick to your guns. When you're right, God is with you, and when he has your back, you will always win.

24-Mar-2014

Hood Economics

DRUGS HAVE PLAYED A BIG PART IN the economy in most inner cities, illegal though it is; unfortunately, this is how a lot of young men and women make money in the urban hoods. I use my home of Newark as a prime example of this. A lot cats in the hood have records, and with a record, getting a halfway decent job can be an adventure especially when you have a limited education. Most people will say to stay in school and get an education, but it's not always that simple. I think back to my junior year in high school; my father's job had closed down, and money was scarce. I even heard him arguing with my mother about me finishing high school; he said how he had to drop out of school in the tenth grade and help his father work in the fields to make ends meet. But for me, dropping out of school was not an option. I was determined; if not for any other reason, I had to finish school and be a better man than him. I did what I had to do to get money, and while I did stay in school, I had my hookups in school. I was able to get a part-time night job in the school and that helped, but I made most of my money selling weed to the white guys who went to the night school. I even tried my hand at the crack trade on weekends when I visited family in East Orange.

Weed was one thing; crack was another. I then saw firsthand what the crack epidemic did to the inner cities; all the pretty sisters who could have been fashion models were turned into crack head prostitutes. There was a young lady named Demetria Davis; she was a couple of years older than me. I believe she was a senior when I was a freshman. I tried my best to talk to her, but all she would do was laugh at a brother. She even made a statement that even if we were the same age, she wouldn't fuck with somebody like me.

All right, fast-forward three years later; she now has a baby and is addicted to crack. She sees me making some change on Eaton Place and William in East Orange; she knows I got that product. Now she wants to talk; she invites me up to her place around the corner. She stayed in a little studio apartment with no real bedroom; she tells me she needs some crack and that she will suck and fuck me right there in her living room, while her little daughter sleeps on the couch a few feet away. I started to go with it just because of what she took me through in the past, plus I hadn't been broke in yet. But I'm a brother who has always had a conscience, and I couldn't bring myself to do it. Besides, at the time, I needed money not sex. Nowadays, I see most of these boys out here just trying to make ends meet when they're out here dealing. Money isn't flowing with the drug boys like it was in my younger days. Back then, even street hustlers on the block were making money. Niggas in that time did a lot of stunting and profiling; I guess that's what made it easy for me to hit up drug spots with my boys a few years later. I hear old heads say back in the day, running numbers was the biggest money-maker in the hood; I guess things were much better then because running numbers can't hurt nobody, but between the dope, the crack, the pills, and all the other shit niggas using to get high, we are losing more and more generations to the drugs or from niggas killing each other. That's why I am inspired to go to my supervisors and propose to them for my next investigative assignment to be on how economics and poor education has a big influence on the narcotic trade in the inner cities. I guess trying to bring awareness to the hoods is my way of getting redemption.

25-Mar-2014

The Importance of Knowing Your Family

THROUGHOUT MY LIFE, I WOULD PERIODICALLY HEAR of a half-sister who lived in North Carolina. I would hear mention of her from my mother, usually when we were alone or around some of her family members. I never heard my father mention her to me, even though she was his child. What little I knew, my father had her when he was still in North Carolina. He moved to Newark when he was seventeen to stay with his aunt. Now I know my father had me with my mom when he was twenty-seven, so I assumed she was a least ten years older than me. I never thought much of the situation growing up, I just considered myself the only child of my mother and father. As I've gotten older and (I believe) a little wiser, I've learned how important it is to know your family members. Not just because getting to know your people is the right thing to do but also because you come across many people and deal with people in different ways; trust me, there are certain ways you don't want to deal with family.

I had never met my sister and never knew anything about her: if she was married, if she had any kids, what kind of job she had. Not knowing anything about her would one day lead to a very uncomfortable moment for me. First, I must tell you the whole story. During my player days, when I was about thirty-three, I was working a side job doing security at a pharmacy downtown. I worked this spot several times before, and there was this younger chick who would come in the pharmacy regularly; she always appeared to be attracted to me and often flirted with me. Her name was Chelsea, and one day,

I asked her for her number, and after speaking to her several times, we went out to dinner. We had a good conversation and appeared to hit it off. We went out a few more times before we finally had sex; keeping it real, the sex was intense. The young lady had me twisted for a minute. At the time, however, I was working a lot, so we just drifted apart, no hard feelings or anything like that; we were just doing our own things.

About seven years later, when my father first became seriously sick (I guess he kinda sensed he was dying), he told me I had a half-sister living at 11 Hill Street in the Hallmark House apartment building. He said her name was Marie Dandrige and that she wasn't married but she did have a daughter. I really didn't pay much attention to what he said at the time. A few months after my father passed, something hit me one day. It just came to me: I really need to get to know my sister. So I went down to the Hallmark building one morning and spoke to the property manager, who I had gotten to know well from when I had the walking post near there. I wrote my cell number down and asked the manager to please advise her who I was and give her my number. A week or so went by before I heard from my sister; we spoke for over an hour. We seemed to hit it off from the start. She soon invited me over. I went over, and we had a great conversation; we then ordered some pizza and continued getting to know each other. Marie told me about her daughter, who also stayed in the building. Before I left, she called upstairs to her daughter, who had just gotten in from work.

When her daughter came downstairs, I looked as if I had seen a ghost; her daughter was in fact Chelsea, the young lady I met years ago in the pharmacy. Wow, was I knocked for a loop. Chelsea had since gotten married and had a child of her own, but you can only imagine how awkward that moment was. We were all able to sit down and rationalize the prior meeting between us. Everyone realized that it wasn't anybody's fault, because we didn't know each other. I can't help but blame my father because he should have made sure his kids knew each other. That's why from this point on, I try my best to know my family members. I don't ever want to have another moment like that.

26-Mar-2014

LIFE IN AND OF ITSELF IS A wonderful teacher. I learned many valuable lessons over the course of my life; one in particular is to keep your enemies close and your so-called family and friends far away. Now don't get me wrong; your family will always be your family, and like Allah says in the holy Koran, do not break the ties of family, and as far as friends go, if you do have real true friends, keep them close to your heart because they are very rare in today's world.

As I stated before, as a young man, I had goals and dreams. There were many times when my so-called family and friends tried to discourage me from following these goals. Hell, my own parents asked me why I wanted to become a police officer; they tried everything to talk me out of it. Some people might say, "Oh, they were just concerned about your safety." I can't call it; only Allah truly knows what is in a person's heart. In my opinion, I think it was all about trying to control me.

But the funny thing about niggas trying to discourage you against achieving your goals is that when, by the grace of the almighty, you do achieve your goal, these same niggas are the first ones looking for a handout or a favor. Niggas who could barely spoke prior to me becoming a cop were now acting like we were the best of friends. Women who wouldn't give me a second look were now sweatin' a nigga. Some people began to say, "Oh, he think he the shit now" or "He arrogant now that he the police." The way I look at it is, if we weren't cool before I became a cop, why should we start trying to be cool now?

My old man was always using my name on the street when he would find himself in some shit, like when another officer would pull him over. Other times, he'd use my name when some of these young thugs on the streets would be ready to get in his ass. A lot of young cats out here on the streets gave me respect because I respected them. I always said this job is just business; it's nothing personal. I once told my father, "You were the main one against me becoming a cop but you the first one to call out my name."

Now that I'm a successful journalist and author, I have a lot of so-called family coming out of nowhere, some of whom I never knew existed, and others I knew about, but they never tried to reach out to me before. So my philosophy applies to them as well: We wasn't cool then, so why be cool now? One family member who I do give props to is my cousin Monique; she has always been for real, God bless her soul. A lot of the family was disappointed in Monique and how she turned out, but regardless of what they may think of her, she was always a down-to-earth person who kept it real. As a child and a young adult, Monique appeared to have it all: She was gorgeous, very smart, a great student, with great personality, and a good athlete. She graduated with honors from Kean College. She went on to get a master's degree in communications. Monique came from good stock; her mother, my aunt Gladys, was an absolute gem of a person. She was one of the best people I ever met in my life, very hard working and with the biggest heart in the world; she believed in me when nobody else did. When she passed away back in 2006, that really hurt me to my inner core. Monique's father, my uncle Harold, was a police officer in East Orange; he was one of my first role models when it came to the whole cop thing.

Monique gave the appearance of someone destined for greatness in life, but somehow, some way, everything went wrong for Monique after college. She started off all right with a good job at Verizon's headquarters in Parsippany, but soon after, she began hanging out with the party crowd; she started getting high and soon lost her job. She left her boyfriend, who was her childhood sweetheart, for a dike chick, and her adult life spiraled downhill until she died about four years ago. I tried to reach out to her, especially after my money got right, but one thing about Monique: She never asked for nothing, no matter what; if anything, she still would ask me if I needed anything and if all was good with me. Yes, that's one thing I can say about cuz: She had my back.

27-Mar-2014

L IKE SO MANY OF US WHO GREW up in the inner city, I have lost several family members in one way or another to the violence in the streets. They were either killed or lost years of their lives due to incarceration. I currently have five family members in jail now. As I stated earlier, I didn't start getting to know my father's side of the family until I got older; now, as I reflect back, maybe my old man did it that way for a reason. That side of the family has some rough street soldiers in it, I must admit. But let's keep it real: We all have choices in life; just because I'm around somebody doesn't mean I have to make the same choices and decisions they make. I just regret not being given a chance to make a choice. One of my cousins on my father's side was named Davon. He was my uncle Leonard's son. We were around the same age, and Davon grew up a few blocks from me on Irving Turner Blvd. Devon was another one I could count on to have my back. We didn't spend a get deal of time around each other coming up, but the time we did spend together was good.

Davon always had a somewhat strained relationship with his father, something we shared in common, but unlike my situation, Uncle Leonard didn't live with him. Like my father, my uncle had some strange ways; he too was a controlling man and considered himself a player, so to speak, which is probably why Davon's mother chose to keep it a boyfriend-girlfriend relationship rather than get married to him. They had an off-and-on relationship for a number of years until one day, my uncle got caught cheating again, and Davon's mom finally had enough. She tried to end the relationship, but this nigga couldn't take no for an answer. He kept on stalking her for several weeks; he even ran off some of her male friends with a baseball bat. Now you can imagine how this troubled my cousin Davon; nobody wants a nigga stalking his mother, even if it is his father. Then came a tragic day in the middle of June. I can still remember getting the phone call at home. Davon had confronted his father the day before, as his father was again harassing his mother. Davon and my uncle had a physical altercation, and my cousin got the better of it. Uncle Leonard went back to his car, got a shotgun, and shot Davon in the stomach. He died shortly afterward. Davon's uncles on his mother's side proceeded to beat the hell out of Leonard. I can't call it, but if you asked me, Uncle Leonard got of light; they should have killed his punk ass.

The whole neighborhood came out for my cousin's wake; that was the first time I saw what has become a trend that is popular in the hood when somebody with a little clout dies: You see people wearing shirts saying "In loving memory of…." I must say, having a family whose name carried weight on the street did help me a lot. Cats be like, "Yo, that's Hood's brother" or "That's Foo's cousin," and other dudes suddenly gave me mad respect, even though I think I more than hold my own. But with all of this being said, with the help of Allah the almighty, I try every chance I get in my free time to counsel young men from my old home, Newark. I try to do whatever I can to get them to put the guns down and pick the books up. The greatest battles are won with the mind. Guns will either cost you your life or years off your life in jail.

28-Mar-2014

A S A COP IN NEWARK, I HAVE seen it all, from some of the most gruesome crime scenes to some the most jubilant celebrations you could think of. Growing up as a youngster in Newark, I often said to myself that as soon as I found a good job and could afford to do so, I would leave the city faster than you could bat an eye, but I stayed in Newark until I retired from the police department. As an officer, I often saw the dark side of Newark (well, hell, I saw a lot of that before I became a cop). In spite of it all, I see Newark as a city with great potential. So many gifted and talented people have come from Newark, and there are still so many young men and women in the city with untapped potential. As a cop, you definitely have to have a thick skin and keep an open mind; out here on these streets, you also have to stay on your toes and keep your eyes open. In spite of it all, after twenty-five years on this job, I'm still more sure than ever that 98 percent of the people I came across on a day-to-day basis were good; it's just that small percent that makes it seem like most are bad because as small as that percent is they can to a lot of harm. Some of the most heart wrenching and disturbing jobs you will encounter as a cop is jobs involving little children. How anyone could harm a little child and in some instances a little baby is mind boggling. I remember a job me and my partner had on South Eighteenth Street we responded to a job of a sexual assault in progress of a three-year-old girl. When we arrived on scene we were immediately approached by the girl's mother, who was hysterical.

She informed us that she had arrived home early that day, and when she entered the house, she heard the music blasting through the halls; when she went upstairs looking for her brother and daughter, she found them in her daughter's room. He was lying next to her daughter, rubbing on her vaginal area. The mother stated she lost it and went downstairs, grabbed a knife, and proceeded to chase her brother around the house. Her brother was able to lock himself in another bedroom and got away by climbing out of the window. After taking the child and mother to Beth Israel Hospital for evaluation, my partner and I were able to get a lead on the whereabouts of her brother, and shortly after that, we were able to capture him. That was one of the most satisfying apprehensions in my career; back then, we didn't have all of these cameras everywhere, so believe me, before he went to jail, a little street justice was served by my partner and I.

One of the best things about being a city cop is you get a first-hand look at many of the changes that occur in the city. You now see nice townhouses where projects once stood (although I must admit, I miss the old projects). The city now has an arena and an arts center, and I have been privileged to see some blueprints of designs for future projects, and they are impressive. There are quite a few things in Newark's past that I do miss, like all of the old movie theaters, where you could see five or six movies for five dollars, and the old drive-in theater. All of the clubs like the Zanzibar and Sensations, the Milk Bar; I swear they had the best cheeseburgers on the planet. In my heart, Newark will always be my home, and in spite of my many difficulties growing up here, I will always love Newark. Now that I have been blessed by the good Lord to be somewhat successful, I have a duty to the city where I was raised. I did my duty as a police officer of course. But much work still needs to be done.

29-Mar-2014

O NE OF MY BIGGEST PET PEEVES, BOTH as a police officer and just a man in general, was drug addicts; now I now there are plenty of people who say that people with addictions have an illness and are the victims in this. I say using drugs is a choice. Victims to me are people who are robbed, are assaulted, or have violent crimes committed against them for no reason whatsoever; those are victims. Junkies make a choice every day to get high. You walk anywhere in the hood and will find these zombies, as I call them, standing around, haunting every neighborhood. These are unproductive people who want nothing out of life except to get their next high. They shack up in empty houses and abandoned buildings with no regard for the owner of the property; they leave bloodstained needles in the parks, in playgrounds, and on sidewalks with no regards for little kids. I remember one day years back, when I still lived on MLK Blvd.; it was a little while after becoming a cop. I was out for a morning run in Green Acres Park; at that time, I didn't like bringing my gun with me when I went running. I think back now, like, what the hell was wrong with me? But anyway, I was out in the park, trying to get my run on, when I came across Darrol Graves, a notorious junkie piece of shit. I was jogging on the track and could see Graves in the bushes, getting ready to shoot up. Growing up around the way like I did, I guess I became used to this. I often saw junkies doing their numbers in the bushes while I was working out or playing ball with friends, so I didn't pay it much attention. Now granted, when I first became a cop, a lot of the guys at my precinct locked up Darrol Graves on a regular basis for panhandling; in fact, that's how a lot of rookies broke their cherry and got their first arrest.

I myself had never arrested Graves; I would just send him on his way. I looked at panhandling as a bullshit arrest; a lot more serious crimes were going on in Newark. But on this particular morning, I don't know if this nigga was high out of his mind or what, but he started to follow me and had a needle hanging out of his arm. I start wondering to myself, *What the hell is going on?*

He started getting closer and closer; finally, I turned around and yelled, "What's up?"

The fool then took the needle out of his arm and started walking toward me. I got into a boxing stance and started moving laterally to avoid that needle (Lord knows whether he had AIDS or what). Finally, I grabbed the biggest rock I can find and threw it at his head. I hit him and stunned him momentarily. I was then able to run out of the park. Keep in mind, I didn't have my weapon or my police radio with me at the time. After leaving the park, I went home and retrieved my weapon and radio. I then went back to the park, looking for Mr. Graves; luckily for my sake and for his ass, I couldn't find him. I made a police report a little later that day, and within a week, he was pick up and arrested. That was one of those events that stays with you forever. It was a learning experience for me, however: to never get to comfortable or complacent with any situation and to be on guard at all times. I saw Mr. Graves a few times after he finished doing his time, and believe me, it wasn't a pleasant experience for him.

During my career, I have caught numerous junkies breaking into the cars and homes of hard-working people who are trying to live a productive life. It doesn't bother me if a person chooses to get high; we are all the captain of our own ship. My problem is when someone else has to suffer a hardship because of another person's habit. My feelings are like this: If you can work and support your habit and not cause anyone else any problems, and if you don't get caught with drugs around me so I don't have to lock your ass up, using drugs is your problem. Just don't make it somebody else's problem. I must admit that one of the most important lessons I have learned in this life is that in order for me to help myself achieve success and to find peace in my life, I had to learn to forgive and let go of certain feelings I carried with me, for example, my feelings toward people with drug addiction. See, I'm getting better; I'm not calling them junkies anymore. I had to learn to practice what I preach; negativity only breeds more negativity. I had to step back and take every person on an individual basis.

Now, don't get it twisted; if someone commits a crime, and I'm on the scene, I'm gonna do my job; being on drugs is definitely not an excuse to commit a crime, but as I became less hard-hearted, I had to admit I was wrong for disagreeing about drug addiction being an illness. It most definitely is. I still feel it is ultimately up to the individual to want and get help for that addiction, but I now know from my own experiences that we are all products of our upbringing and environments, to some extent. I know I was (and still am, in many ways), but through education and proper upbringing, you learn how to adjust and get around your circumstances. When I took time to talk to some of the people I arrested who are addicted to drugs, I began to gain a better understanding of what they were really dealing with on a day-to-day basis; with a lot of them, drugs are just half the problem. A lot of them also suffer from depression and other mental illnesses.

30-Mar-2014

ORKING OUT HAS PLAYED A CRITICAL ROLE in my life. The number one reason for my successes and well-being in life is my unyielding faith in God. But working out has always kept me grounded, and it's always been an outlet for all of the turbulence I've had to deal with in this lifetime. Many days prior to being a cop (and even more days while I was a cop), I carried a great deal of tension and frustration with me. Usually, however, after a good workout session, my tension was relieved, and I could think about whatever problem I had with a much clearer mind. That's why I try to advise most of these young boys out here who are always fighting and getting into confrontations on the street to start going to the recreation centers where they have gyms and to get involved in sports because those activities are great outlets for your aggression.

For me, boxing was my outlet, and even now in my older age, I still try to hit the gym as much as I can. Punching the bag is great exercise and a good safe outlet for your aggression. Now by no means am I one of these muscle-head guys out here; I've always tried to work out, but I just recently got seriously into the nutritional aspect of conditioning, which is another reason why I thank God so much for giving me the strength to work out, because Lord knows my diet hasn't always been the best. Yet in spite of my diet, with Allah's help and a pretty consistent workout routine, I have maintained pretty good health. As a child, unfortunately, like many African American youths at that time, my parents only took me to the doctor when I was sick, which was hardly ever. So I never went for yearly physicals. Like many black males after a certain age, I developed high blood pressure; for some reason, it plagues many blacks in this country, even if they live a relatively healthy lifestyle. Another important reason I keep getting my workout on is because even though I haven't been able to escape high blood pressure, I have by the grace of God been able to keep it well controlled over the years from working out. My doctor has me on a very low dosage of medication, and my blood pressure is very stable. But I'm not satisfied with that; one day soon, I hope to be off of blood pressure medication period.

Back to the subject of boxing: Now, this is just my feeling on the matter of all of these killings and shootings that are out of hand in the inner cities. Since these gang bangers and thugs have so much hostility in them, why not try boxing? It a great way to release your anger, and you won't go to jail. There are still boxing gyms in most inner cities, and over the years, these gyms have helped a number of young men with violent pasts turn their lives around. I remember one day in my middle teens, I was on my way to the gym; it was a hot summer afternoon. I had just gotten off of the bus and still had to walk three blocks to get to the gym. There was a group of three dudes standing on the block; I noticed that they kept staring at me when I got off the bus. I tried to ignore them, but I had a funny feeling they were about to try something, and they started following me. I started to walk faster; I knew once I got to the gym, a few fighters would be in there training. Once I began to speed up, they sped up. So I took off running; they chased me to the gym. Once I got inside, a boxer saw I looked startled; I advised him what had just happened. He went outside along with a professional fighter named James Dale; they went out, confronted the three dudes, and challenged them to come into the gym and box me, one at a time. The three accepted the challenge, so they came in, we put the gloves on, and got it on. The next day, when they saw me on my way to the gym, they walked up to me and shook my hand. See, back then you could get a fair one.

31-Mar-2014

BELIEVE ME WHEN I TELL YOU CHANGE is a good thing a wonderful thing. Life without change is like stagnant water; it just stays there, dead and lifeless. I used to be very resistant to change. I guess it came from the way I was raised. My parents were not very creative people; they pretty much did the same things every day. Don't get me wrong; consistency is a good thing. Being resistant to change, however, is not a good thing. Life itself and the world around us is always changing and evolving, maybe not always for the best, but changing nonetheless. That's why we must change and adapt with the world. Anyone who cannot adapt will soon be extinct. Like I said before, I had been complacent for much of my younger days; even when I became a cop, I was just happy to be on the job. I was happy just living my life in a certain comfort zone. I regret not making rank on the job. I also regret not going for an investigative position; in my opinion, it is good to re-create yourself every so often. By that I mean being known for doing more than just one thing. My job as a police officer was my foundation, and it did lead me to other things after I retired. I just wish I had tried different things while I was still on the job.

Maybe it's just a pipe dream, but another thing I regret is not pursuing a pro boxing career on the side. I was fortunate enough to get a steady shift in my fourth year on the job. (Most of the patrol division rotated on an around-the-clock schedule), and I could have worked out a training routine with the shift I had. Who knows, I might even have been a contender or a champion. My guess is that we all have some regrets from the past.

As a child growing up, I never left my area much; my parents never took a real vacation. My father's idea of a vacation was going down to his old town in Henderson, North Carolina. We would go down there occasionally when his mother, my other grandmother, was living. But even those visits were few and far between. I think I may have seen my grandmother a total of five times before she passed. Now that I think about it, as a child, the only areas I saw were in Newark (of course), with occasional trips to East Orange and Irvington. Living life in that manner doesn't help you to fully grow as a person; you never really see anything different. Once you're physically out of a certain environment, you start to see how beautiful this world is and how much it has to offer. Even though it took me awhile after I became a cop to get over my complacency, I thank Allah for that job because it gave me the financial resources to travel and see other places. I am most thankful for my new career as a journalist. I now travel the world and meet many interesting people. I am now more humble and grateful for the life Allah has given me because in spite of my past problems, I now see after traveling to different parts of the world how many people have had it much worse than me.

1-Apr-2014

FROM TIME TO TIME YOU HAVE HEARD me mention my faith which is al-Islam, which means the submission to the will of almighty God, Allah. Islam has saved me in so many ways; it has kept me sane when I thought I was going insane, and it has kept me grounded when it seemed as though things were spinning out of control. I'll be the first one to admit I haven't always been the best Muslim. But I won't be too hard on myself; we all have sins, no matter what our faith is. The key, however, is it's not about how many times you fall but how often you rise from adversity. Growing up, I always believed in God. That's one thing about most African American families in the hoods; no matter how bad our situation is or how rough our hood is, we keep a strong faith in God, whether we call him Allah, Jehovah, or Jesus. Even though my parents instilled a belief in God in me, I really didn't go to church much with them. I went to a Catholic grammar school at St. Mary's, and part of the curriculum was religion as a class (it was the Catholic religion, of course) and would go to the church every so often for Mass. That was pretty much my exposure to religion growing up.

When I got old enough, I wanted to find a faith of my own. I wanted to gain a better knowledge of the creator and find a sense of direction for my life; my mother and father were both Baptist, so I tried several different Baptist churches. I never quite found what I was looking for in the church. Of course, I have nothing against the church. I feel like this: There is only one God, and we all have our own way of serving and believing in him. The key is that you believe. When I found Islam, I knew I had found my way. I found a religion that touched my heart and commanded my attention. I found Islam to be the religion of truth.

My first introduction to Islam was through the Nation of Islam under the leadership of Minister Louis Farrakhan; NOI was a strong organization that built character and discipline. The Nation of Islam has been extremely instrumental in changing the lives of many young African American men and women. It gives them direction and a sense of purpose in their lives; the nation stresses good morale conduct. I valued my time in the nation of Islam, but at that time in my life, I was looking for something more spiritual. A few years later, I took shahada (a declaration of faith in Islam) at the mosque on Branford Place in Newark. I began to study the sunnah of the Prophet Muhammad, who Muslims believe was the last prophet sent to earth by almighty God. In this study, I found the spiritual enlightenment that I was searching for.

As I have grown older, I now realize the importance of having the proper balance of the spiritual, physical, and (most importantly) mental, and the reason I say mentally is most important is because everything starts with the mind; if the mind ain't right, nothing will be right. Now this again is just my feelings on the matter. I know Muslims of all denominations may disagree with me on this, but in my opinion, a lot of Muslims in this area only want to deal with the spiritual side of Islam. Islam encompasses every aspect of life. The Koran speaks about science education and covers every aspect of human existence. Look at a subject like quantum physics; some religions conflict with this and other aspects of sciences. When you get a true understanding of Islam, you will see that it doesn't conflict with science. Even though taking shahada and converting to a more orthodox version of Islam helped me spiritually, there was still something missing. I really began to balance everything out when I began to study at the Muhammad Mosque on South Orange Avenue in Newark. I had some family history at that mosque. Some of my family members attended the mosque back when it was Temple Twenty-Five under the leadership of the original nation of Islam, which was then led by the honorable Elijah Muhammad.

Nowadays the mosque follows the more traditional version of Islam and is under the leadership of Iman Warith Deen Muhammad, the son of Elijah Muhammad. Iman Muhammad's teachings put a lot of emphasis on the human intellect. He taught us how import it is to be rational and sane in your study of Islam. He taught us the true measure of a man and especially a leader is in his intellect and his compassion for all of humanity. Every day that I'm blessed by Allah to wake up is both a blessing and a challenge; the blessing is that I woke up, but I know there will be challenges every day. I should already know I've damn sure had my share in the past. But I now I say bring on the challenges. I look forward to them. I'm now armed with knowledge of my Lord and a focused mind; bring it on!

2-Apr-2014

As I have gotten older, I now do a lot of reflecting on my past, not from a negative way though. I now think about the positive that came from periods in my life that at the time I thought were so dreadful. Don't get me wrong; some of those situations I wouldn't wish on my worst enemy, but God is so good, and he brought me through it. I'm a living testament to the saying "What doesn't kill you will make you stronger." I now believe all those trying moments were needed to make me the person that I am and prepare me for what paths the Lord above had made for me.

My whole outlook is totally different at this point in my life. I no longer have bad days; every day, every moment is a blessing. Of course, things are not going to go your way every day, but that's cool; just because the day starts off bad doesn't mean the whole day is going to be bad. I remember one day in particular; I started the day as usual with morning roll call. After that I had a court case in municipal court at nine o'clock; court went smoothly then after that I went back to my command for a vehicle. I took vehicle 318; when I took the car, I saw that the gas gauge was almost empty; as usual, the night crew didn't put fuel in the vehicle. So I went up to the fire house to fuel up; when I got there, I ended up making a very stupid move: I put diesel in the tank instead of gas. Wow, I said to myself, I really fucked up now. But this happened later in my career when I developed a stronger, more confident mind-set. When I was younger, this would have stressed me out so much that my whole day would have been ruined. On top of that, when I went back and took another vehicle out, I locked myself out of the car shortly afterward.

No problem; I just continued my day. I was determined to finish the day on a good note.

Later that afternoon, a few hours before I was due to get off, I pulled over a car on Broad and Market with Massachusetts plates. I pulled them over for making an illegal turn at the intersection; it started off as a normal pull-over. The driver of the car failed to exhibit a registration card so I ran the license plate. The dispatcher advised me that the car was wanted in connection to a murder back in Massachusetts, and the owner of the car was wanted for murder. I then called for backup, and after units responded, I arrested the driver. Follow-up investigations showed that the driver was in fact the owner, and he was not only wanted for murder, he was also on the FBI's most-wanted list. What started off as a bad day for me at work ended up with me getting a Class A Award. After a day like that, I know this to be true, whether you are speaking about certain days or life in general: It's not always important how it starts but how it ends.

3-Apr-2014

IN THE LAST FEW YEARS OF MY career as a cop and shortly after I retired, I was a little apprehensive. I wasn't quite sure what to expect, even though I had continued my education while I was a cop. I had just spent the last twenty-five years of my adult life as a police officer, I was thinking to myself, *Damn, now I got to go out and get a real job (lol).* I decided to just go out there, keep thinking positive, and put my faith in God, as I have always done. Little did I know what wonderful things where awaiting me. As the saying goes, when one door closes, another one opens. That wonderful chapter in my life as a police officer was over, but now an even more beautiful chapter was opening. I loved being a cop; for all of the stress and aggravation I got from the job, I still loved it, and if I had to do it all over again, I wouldn't hesitate.

My new job now as a journalist is the icing on the cake. With this new career, I not only make a considerable amount more money, I'm now finally getting my chance to do the investigative work that I dreamed about early in my career as a cop.

As an investigative journalist, I'm now able to thoroughly investigate my assignment without having to worry about time restraints, political ramifications, or departmental bureaucracy. This new job is one of the major factors why I changed my outlook on the way I grew up; after being on assignment in Africa, Indonesia, and certain parts of the former Soviet Union, I began to see for myself how some youths have it way tougher than I did. Yeah, of course I saw pictures of most of this growing up on television, but the effect of seeing these things in person is stunning.

Journalism is a field of work where you can open up and be expressive. In this field, when you create controversy and ruffle some feathers, it is a good thing. I used to think the thugs in Newark were rough, but I'm here to tell you, I an assignment in Brazil and in Jamaica. I did a feature on two drug cartels, one in each country, and after finishing those assignments, I saw what being gangster is really about; cats in Newark are puppies compared to those boys. They take the term "ruthless killers" to a whole different level.

In some instances, this job can be more dangerous than being a cop; some of the neighborhoods I have to go into to cover some of these stories are ten times worse than Newark. At least in Newark, if I got on the radio and called for help, I had a force coming behind me; of course, I get security when I have to investigate in the areas, but in those neighborhoods, you would need an army if things got out of control.

I must admit, I do enjoy the adventure of it all. I get a rush from the suspense and the danger. Luckily, my beautiful wife is there to remind me that I now have a family plus financial stability from my book sales, so there's no need to be so reckless. I try to explain to her to just be patient with me. I can't help it; my entire life has been reckless (lol).

4-Apr-2014

THE GREATEST JOB I HAVE AND EVER will have is my job as a husband and a father; my family is everything to me. They are the reason for me being who I am today. My wife, Jennifer, is my better half for real; she had helped to complete me in every way. My son, Amir, is the apple of my eye; he is the biggest reason why I push so hard to be as successful as I can in all of my endeavors, so that I can provide a strong foundation for my family financially. I want to be an example for him of how you can achieve success through faith and hard work, regardless of your circumstances. I'm a role model for real now.

5-Apr-2014

IN CLOSING, I AM NOW SO THANKFUL for everything my Lord has given me. I've had a blessed life. Indeed, the good Lord must look out for fools and babies because he has certainly looked out for me. I hope my story can inspire someone out there, especially someone who has grown up in conditions similar to mine. Never give up on this life you have. Every day you wake up, there's something for you to do, something that can be accomplished, something to be learned. Don't waste this time here on earth. Make goals for the future, and every day, take a step (even if it is a baby step) toward your goals; in fact, it's good to set goals every day. Just as long as you wake up every day with a sense of purpose. For years, I just survived; I thought I was living. I saw the world through shallow eyes; I wasn't living up to my full potential. Growing up the way I did, you're just happy to make it from one day to the next. And if you do make it to adulthood and get a good job, you think you are on top of the world. Let's keep it real: Coming out of the hood, that is a great accomplishment. I take nothing away from it, but I'm here to tell you that you can be more. I'm living proof of it. I once thought I was cursed; even as a child, I lost so many people who were close to me. I had to deal with a lot before I was even fifteen years old. I have still managed to rise from this, in spite of the pain and despair. If I can do it, so can you. I know this is a fictional story, but those who are able to read through the lines know there is plenty of truth in fiction, if you know what I mean. My advice is, keep the faith, keep your mind right (because that's where it all starts from), and never give up, in spite of those around you. You owe it to yourself to give everything you have toward your goals. To live without trying, you might as well be dead. You have many choices in this world, no matter what your circumstances are. America is not perfect, but it is the greatest nation on earth and the best thing going. Faith in God and a strong, determined mind can take you places you never dreamed were possible. Redemption is possible.

6-Apr-2014

For most of my early life, I was very uncomfortable in meeting people; it took me awhile in most cases to get comfortable enough to open up, even around my family, let alone people I didn't know too well. While I am by no means a physiologist, I believe most of this came from my parents keeping me sheltered for much of my youth; some parents believe strongly in those old-fashioned ways of being dominating figures in your life, no matter how old you are. There are a lot of people who may think this way (in particular, many black families), but I can say this without hesitation: That way of thinking is bullshit. At some point, all human beings must become their own person; too much parental smothering will hurt the child's social development.

For the longest time, I felt very uncomfortable in situations where I had to address people. I struggled badly with putting my words together; I guess this is probably why I had so much trouble with the ladies when I was younger. That gift of gab, as they say, is an important weapon to have in this life. It can help you out in so many ways, not just with the ladies but with job interviews, correspondence, and business matters. It can be a useful tool to have in life, period. No man or woman is an island, so good people skills are a must. The problem with a lot of old-fashioned black parents is that they want to relive their lives through their kids. You only live once on this earth, so be all you can be in your life and live it to the fullest, and after that, sit your ass down and let the next generation live their lives.

The one thing that helped me overcome my problem was becoming a cop. I dealt with so many people on a day-to-day basis,

I became a lot more comfortable dealing with strangers. That's why I'm a big proponent for young black men, especially those who may be somewhat quiet and reserved, to either give the military a try or get into law enforcement. You will gain valuable life experiences from either of these fields, and it will help you develop your confidence.

7-Apr-2014

I HEARD IT SAID MANY TIMES THAT THE best things in life are free. Well, I'm here to tell you that's a crock of shit. Don't you believe it. In today's world, if there's anything for free, please show it to me. Maybe at one time people did something for free, but I must say, from my experience at least, in forty-plus years on this earth, I've never seen anything given for free. Even my own parents were usually looking for something in exchange for a favor. Growing up in the ghetto, most of us lived by the barter system; in other words, there's no robbery in a fair exchange, a tick for a tack, give me this for that. However you say it, it adds up to the same thing; nothing is given for free. I remember one day during one of my broke days as a cop, my car stalled on me on Route 22 in Newark (a very busy highway). I had just spent my money on a few electrical items and left my credit cards at home. So I called my department's tow company to see if I could get an emergency tow, as a courtesy. They said they would come for me; I explained my financial situation to them, and they said it wouldn't be a problem. So I waited and waited and waited; four hours later, they finally came to get me. Don't get me wrong; I appreciated them helping me out, but damn, after waiting out on the highway for four hours in the middle of December, I was done.

There is another old saying: money talks and bullshit walks, and I now know that holds true to almost everything. Keeping it real, it's even hard to get some pussy for free. Most sisters don't wanna give you some for nothing; they used to even say, "No money, no honey." I hate to admit it, but during my single days, some of the best pussy was the one I paid for. You know why? Because when a chick is trying to make some money, she gonna do a good job. Whether she suckin' or fuckin', she wants you to come back so she can keep a steady money flow. I'm just keeping it real. All in all, the way I see it, you're probably better off paying for whatever; at least when it's done, you don't owe nobody anything. Some of my boys say they are not trying to pay a chick for some ass; I asked them who are they tryna convince by saying that. Themselves? They must be, because that's damn sure not foolin' me; that may work when you're young in high school and in college, but once chicks become adults, sisters in particular, and they realize the power of that pussy, you're givin' up something, in some way, shape, or form. You might get it from a chick who's naïve and don't know the game, but even a chick like that will catch on once her home girls start getting her up to speed on the game. Yep, once she learns how to use that hole to get what she wants, it's all over. Only other time a bitch try and give it up for free is when she gets older and that body starts sagging and the pussy ain't quite as tight as it used to be; in other words, she don't think she the shit no more. Then she might give up that stink hole for free. People are gonna be people until they are in the ground, and believe me when I tell you, ain't nothing for free. Everybody is chasing something.

8-Apr-2014

FEAR OFTEN HELD ME BACK. NOW WHEN I think back, I ask myself, "What the hell was I afraid of?" I once heard of a saying that went like this: Life and its problems are only as bad as you perceive them. When I was younger, I was afraid of my own shadow. Even though I often fought on the streets, I can't remember a time when I wasn't constantly looking over my shoulder when I came out of the house. I remember once on my way to grammar school, I saw a group of guys and girls walking down the street; they looked like project kids. You could always tell the kids from the projects by the way they walked, talked, and acted. As soon as I saw them, I immediately crossed to the other side of the street; one of the girls noticed me and said, "Damn, look at that big-head punk nigga over there," and they began to laugh at me. Back then, as a youngster hearing things like that bothered me; my pride was hurt. Now as an adult, I see things a little differently. I can now be proud that I made the right decision; in life, there will be times when you have to just walk away. I can now see a much broader picture; just look at how my life has turned out compared to theirs. A couple of those dudes are in and out of jail; a few others are dead. Two of the girls are now strung out on that shit, and the girl who made the remark about me is now selling her ass on Clinton Avenue.

It took me forever to learn this (especially after I got older; after sixteen, I wasn't scared of nothing, and then I wanted to fight the world). But there will be many times in life where it's best to just walk away. Allah the almighty has protected me in so many ways; mainly, he has protected me from myself. As a young adult, I was very hostile; it didn't take much at all to set me off. One thing I definitely believed in was revenge. The Lord above kept me out of jail and saved me from messing up my record because if I had, I would have never become a police officer.

Over the last half of my career, I really learned humility because times have changed with new technology and a much different mind-set of the general public. With all the cameras and people with cellphones, you really have to be on point with what you do out here as a police officer. I began to look at my job as if I were an actor; I always imagined that the camera was shooting me (lol). But I guess you could say life in general is just one big stage and all of us are just actors in one way, shape, or form; it's just that with life, you kind of write your own script. As I'm older now, my eyes and heart are more open. I used to carry a lot of hard feelings toward my old man, but now I can honestly say he played a role in shaping me to be who I am today. Everything happens for a reason, and for every action, there is an equal and opposite reaction. While I'm still not cool with how he tried to use me, I think back that maybe if he hadn't been hard on me in certain ways when I was younger and kept me away from certain people, maybe things would not have turned out quite so well.

I may have ended up dead or in jail, like so many people on that side of the family. One of my cousins, Antonio, is currently in Trenton State Prison; I can't even imagine that many years behind bars. He has been in there since he was sixteen years old. I remember when I was about thirteen, my father took me over to his uncle's house. I had only seen my father's grandson, my cousin Tony, maybe three times in my life. Tony always liked me, but he had a strange way of showing it: Every time we were around each other, he would try to rough me up; he said I looked a little soft to him, so he wanted to toughen me up. So on that particular day, Tony asked my father could I go around the corner with him and a few of his friends; my father said no, he told me that area wasn't for me. I remember Uncle Rodger told my pops that he should let me go. He told my pops treating me like a baby was what was making me soft. My pops stuck by his guns and said no. Anyway, a few hours later, when we were going home, Tony still wasn't back yet. On the way back home, we saw a police crime scene in front of a store a few blocks away. We didn't pay it any attention; we saw crime scenes all of the time. Well, anyway, a few days later, Uncle Rodger said that my cousin Antonio was just picked up by police in connection with a double homicide. My father told me that he had a funny feeling about Antonio, and he worried about me being around him. When I think about it now, fear can be a good thing; it saved me that day.

9-Apr-2014

T HIS ONE IS ALL ABOUT THE LADIES. Until I met my lovely wife, Jennifer, I considered my relationships with the ladies to be failures. I never thought I would ever get married or settle down. I believed most of these young ladies were just good for one thing and one thing only: sex. Most of my past relationships were failures, and I'm man enough to admit that a lot of it had to do with me. I was one of the biggest whores you could meet. Once I had finally gotten broke in, I went on a rampage. When I woke up in the morning, after morning prayer, the first thing on my mind was sex (safe sex, of course, but sex nonetheless). I really had little respect for most sisters. I carried a lot of anger from the past. I remembered how sisters used to treat a brother when I was younger, and even though I love her to death, I had a controlling mother. So you can imagine how fucked up I was in the head. Let's keep it real; a lot of black women are very controlling if you let them, and I wasn't having it. I had been controlled and pushed around enough. When I was in my twenties and thirties, I would cuss a bitch out before you could take your next breath. It almost cost me at work a few times; I came very close to having a couple of domestic violence cases. Nothing physical. As much as the women could get on my nerves, I would never put my hands on a woman; I'd rather just move on. It was just when I was younger I would give them a piece of my mind before I would move on.

I started to change as I was approaching thirty. One relationship I had was with a Muslim sister named Halima; she was tall and attractive. She worked as a hairstylist, and in her spare time she modeled clothes for Islamic women. We were together for over a year. It was a good relationship most of the time; she was five years older than me, which is no big deal, but she was the type of sister who knows it all. I couldn't tell her anything, so you already know what it led to: I cursed her out. A few hours later, baby girl made a police report on me for harassment. After my internal affairs got wind of that report, I was placed on desk duty for about a year. The restraining order she had on me was dropped right away; the judge must have known it was bullshit. I still had to go through the whole routine. I lost my gun for a year; they said it was supposed to be a cooling off period. I worked the administrative part of policing for a year as well. It was all good; I learned quite a bit about how the department works from the inside.

A few months after the incident, Halima met some African Muslim brother, and she married him a couple of months later. I thought, *Wow, so quick after we had broken up.* It made me think she was dealing with the nigga all along, even when we were together. Oh well, only God knows, but life goes on. I soon forgave her and asked her to please forgive me for my foolishness and bad behavior.

Some time passed, and we became cool after that. I'm glad we made amends for our past problems because tragedy hit just a few years down the road. She and her husband went through a bad breakup and divorce. Her ex became upset with her and began to stalk her. It was during that period of my life I began to see how life can take a 360-degree turn in the blink of an eye. Halima was working at the Gateway Center on Mulberry Street in Newark, and I just happened to be assigned a walking post that covered that area. One day, I was out on my daily patrol and saw a woman running down the street and a guy running close behind, so I started running and got on my police radio to call for additional help. I gave the location over the air, and units responded within minutes. When I caught up to them, I could see it was Halima and her ex-husband. She explained to me that he had just tried to get her to get into his car, and when she refused, he punched her in the face. She told me she managed to get away and start running.

I locked him up and helped her get a temporary restraining order. Halima was very grateful to me for helping her; I told her I was just doing my job. He ex was eventually released, and the story came to a sad end several months later. Halima suddenly disappeared. She was missing for two months, and her ex-husband hadn't been seen either. I prayed for the best, but in my heart, I knew what had probably happened. Halima's body was found a little before Thanksgiving in back of an abandoned warehouse in East Orange, New Jersey. After a yearlong hunt for her ex, he was apprehended by US Marshals in Texas. I learned a valuable lesson from all of that: Treat people good while they are here, and don't hold grudges over nonsense; life is too short. I'm glad I was able to make up with her and gain closure before her sudden death.

10-Apr-2014

MY YEARS AT ESSEX COUNTY COLLEGE WERE some of the best in my life. I loved going to school at night. The college at night had a whole different vibe about it than the day school. It almost seemed like they dimmed the lights a little at night. I loved being around educated and motivated brothers and sisters who were trying to better themselves. The only drawback at this time of my life was that I was always broke. Between paying for my college credits and having to pay my sorry ass old man rent, I never had any money.

I also stayed in great shape then. When I worked at the car dealer, that job could be physically exhausting, and of course I couldn't afford a car then, so I either walked everywhere or caught the bus. My schedule during the week was demanding. I worked from eight to five and then went to school, usually between six and ten o'clock, and all of this with no car. I look back now with great pride because all of my hard work paid off. During my college days, I met many influential people like City Councilman John Harris; he was one of the counselors at the college. He helped students find jobs while in school and after they graduated. He was very inspiring and helped me out during my evaluation period prior to joining the police.

Going to the college also gave me an escape from other aspects of my life, like going home to Brick Towers and my fucked-up father. But no matter what, I still had to return home at some point.

I remember coming home from school one summer evening; that day, I got out at eight o'clock because one of my classes had been canceled. When I got to my building, I saw police picking up lots of yellow tape from the front of the building. Of course, growing up in the Bricks, this was unfortunately something that you got used to. When I got upstairs, my mother informed me that my boy Donald Reid, from the apartment down the hall, had been in a fight earlier that day and was stabbed to death. This type of shit happens much too often in the hood, so you start to get tough skin. It hurts at first, of course; then the next day comes, and it's back to the same every-day grind. At least I had college in my life; that, along with Islam, helped ease those painful times. That's why I can't stress enough to youngsters how important it is to continue your education after you get out of high school. The college campuses in Newark are like an oasis in the desert. No matter how gloomy the inner city may have looked in the surrounding areas, and no matter how much crime was going on in the rest of the city, the college campuses are like a city within the city. It is an escape, even if just a temporary one, for some-one living in hard circumstances. I regret not being able to live on campus and experience the full effect of college life, but I had to get out and make the doughnuts. I had the same dreams as most young college students. I wanted to finish school, get my diploma, get a good job, move up the ladder, become successful, and get married. You know, the good old American dream, or should I say, the good old white American dream? Listen to me now; I am by no means a racist. My high school was racially mixed, and I got along well with everybody. I'm not my father's son in that way, but I keep it real. Most of us who grow up in the hood have nightmares, not dreams; we're happy just to wake up from one day to the next. John Strong, a white guy I worked with at the car dealer, was a good man, a damn good man. He was only three years older than me and worked as a mechanic. He lived in the Vailsburg section of Newark and had a big influence on my decision to go to college. John was an intelligent, level-headed guy, and being around him had a calming effect on me. John once asked me where I saw myself by the time I was thirty; now mind you, I was eighteen when he asked me. My answer to him was, "Hopefully, I'll still be alive."

12-Apr-2014

RAGEDY HAS FOUND ITS WAY INTO MY life on many occasions. I've heard it said that into each life some rain must fall, but damn, sometimes it's like my life has been a whole freakin' typhoon. Even at a young age, I used to think back, like, *Can I ever get a break?* First, my grandmother died when I was three. Then my great aunt Beatsie passed when I was seven, and then my cousin Davon, and so many others were lost to jail. While all of this has made me stronger as a person, certain scars last forever. The holy Koran makes it clear when it says to live as though tomorrow is not promised to you, but to also live as though you are going to live forever. I now try to give my all every day, no matter what. As a ten-year-old, I remember my mother getting the phone call from my aunt Dawn that her husband had just shot himself in the head, right in front of her. Believe me, as a cop in Newark, I've seen and heard it all, but I still get chills up my spine when I think about that night. Ironically, my uncle had also been a police officer in Newark. He was also one of the inspirations for my decision to become a police officer. With so many tragedies combined with the fucked-up area I grew up in, I often felt like crawling under a rock and just hiding. Life doesn't work like that, however; there are no time-outs, and you can't run from every obstacle.

With all of these tragedies, I spent my fair share of time at wakes and funerals. Even when we were in our twenties, I used to hear some of my friends say how they had never been to a wake or funeral. Hearing something like this was foreign to me because Lord knows I had been to my share. When I was a child, after being exposed to so many dead bodies, I was often scared to go to sleep alone at night.

I think back now and laugh about that because now from my experience living in and patrolling the hood, I now know one thing for sure: the ones you better watch out for are these fools who are living and breathing, not a dead person. Believe this: Once you die in this world and they take out your heart, lungs, and all that good stuff, you ain't ever getting back up again. See you in the next life.

13-Apr-2014

BEING A COP IN NEWARK (OR ANYWHERE else, for that matter) is a thankless job for real. One minute, you're a person's best friend when you're helping them or doing what they want. Then in the next breath, you're the biggest piece of shit going when you have to enforce the law on them. When I first became a cop, working in patrol on the street was the thing to be; you were respected, and people in general looked out for you. But toward the end of my career, all of that changed. People were much less respectful of the police, and few would look out for you. I saw a lot of cops who were aggressive go-getters when they started the job turn into lazy, good-for-nothing pieces of shit, just looking for a paycheck every two weeks. Can't really say I blame them the way things are nowadays; who wants to risk losing their homes or pensions over bullshit? From day one of the academy, the instructors told us that once you become a cop, you are now as close as you would probably ever come to going to jail. All it takes is one slip-up, one miscalculation; just one honest mistake can cost you everything.

I remember one time in particular when I first came on the job. Me and my partner Kim went on a dispatched assignment on Oxford Street; it was a call about two suspicious males looking into a house. When we arrived on scene, we were met by two other rookie officers, Costello and Martin. We noticed that the lock on the front door was damaged, but the door was still locked, so the first thing we did was ring the bell. When no one answered, we advised the dispatcher to call to the Emergency Services Unit (ESU), in case we had to make an entry to the house and see if anyone was in there who wasn't supposed to be there. Before Kim and I finished making notifications,

Costello and Martin had picked the lock and were headed up the stairs. We called them back and told them we should wait for the ESU unit.

Now by this time, a neighbor walked over to see what was going on, and after talking with him, Costello and Martin followed him into the house. A few minutes later, the owners of the house came out and told us that he and his wife had damaged the locks themselves after they had locked themselves out of the house. So later on that day, after everything was straightened out and all officers had left the scene, Kim and I got called into Internal Affairs. When we got there, the sergeant said that the owners of the house we checked on earlier claimed that five thousand dollars was missing from one of the rooms in the house, and the neighbor had told them the only ones in the house were the police. Kim and I informed the sergeant that we never put one foot in the house; the neighbor was a liar because he entered the house with Costello and Martin. We spent a better part of that tour being interviewed about that job. I wasn't worried about it; I knew I did nothing wrong, and when you're right, God is with you. All officers were cleared of any wrongdoing. But it's just the principle of having to deal with the BS. That just goes to show how easy it is to get in trouble on this job. That along with the danger of this job; some people may think I'm crazy for saying this, but it was still the best job I ever had.

14-Apr-2014

Y OU OFTEN SEE COP SHOWS ON REALITY TV. These shows come from the real-life experiences of cops around the country. What puzzles me is why, after all of this time, nobody has ever made a reality TV show about a place I call my home away from home, Broad and Market. Broad and Market has been a part of my life and my career for as long as I can remember. Even before I was a cop, Broad and Market was my life. After taking shahada and becoming Muslim, I would often hang with some brothers from the mosque; a lot of them, especially back in those days, were street peddlers, and one of their primary locations was the Broad and Market area. Things were a little better on Broad and Market in those times. Make no mistakes about it, the drugs and all the other hustles still went on; they have been going on forever in one way or another. The difference was whatever was done, was done more discreetly and with more respect.

After becoming a cop, I was often assigned to patrol Broad and Market. I didn't think anything of it at the time, since my precinct included that area. Little did I know that this was just the beginning of the assignment that would become the focal point from most of my career. About a year or so after I became a cop, I started working side jobs for extra money. And my first side job was at CC's Department Store, located right at the corner of Broad and Market. It was a women's department store, which was just fine with me; I was a young man in my mid-twenties, single with no kids; I was like a kid in a candy store. I got paid often working that spot, and I'm not just talking about my salary, if you know what I mean. I had plenty of fun working there, but it was still Broad and Market, where things just come to you or happen right in front of you. Besides having fun, I made my share of arrests while working that store. My precinct commander must have noticed the number of arrests I had over there, so Broad and Market soon became my permanent assignment. I can say without hesitation that the intersection of Broad and Market made me the officer that I am.

Broad and Market is the busiest intersection in the state of New Jersey. I believe it is second only to Times Square in New York among populated intersections in the tristate area. You see everything you can think of on Broad and Market. There are dudes who have sold drugs for decades out there. They get locked up, do a little time, stay away a little while, but they somehow find their way back to Broad and Market. I guess I must be a kindred soul with these guys because no matter how many times I get reassigned to another area, I still find my way back to Broad and Market. I was told by one of my captains that I had the most arrests ever in one year at Broad and Market, so I guess that answers the question of why the department had such a fascination with me and that intersection.

One thing I can say is that after working this area for so many years, I have gained the respect of most of the citizens I encountered. I have damn sure had my share of confrontations out here, but I guess that's needed from time to time to get your respect. Yep, Broad and Market has been like a second home for me. Broad and Market is known as the heart of the Bricks; out here, I'm simply known as Hazel Eyes.

15-Apr-2014

I'M NOT EVEN FIFTY YEARS OLD, BUT it feels as though I have lived about one hundred years. I have seen so much and dealt with so many situations. Sometimes, I feel a little burned out, but those feelings pass quickly because there is so much life yet to live. I still have to make a difference in a few more lives. I still have some more lives to save, and I damn sure have a lot more money to make (lol). Back in the day, I would have also said "a lot more women to meet," but I'm now a happily married man and no longer think that way. I must admit that being faithful is a challenge out here; the women really do come at you a lot harder when you have somebody. When I was single, I used to hear married men say it was like that all of the time. I didn't pay much attention then. Now, I sometimes have to literally run from the ladies.

I can't rule out one other factor that may contribute to my current popularity with women. I'm now in the 1 percent, which certainly makes me a bigger fish in the pond. As a cop, I thought I had a big come-up with the ladies, but now with so many women reading my articles and books, it's like I went from being a Cadillac to being a Rolls-Royce. Hey, let's keep it real; like I said earlier, money talk and BS walks. I stay grounded, though; when God blesses you with a good wife, family, and wealth, you better stay humble and appreciate it. And the best way to ensure appreciation is to not be greedy. Not everything that looks good is good for you. I have too much to lose to lose it all for some pussy. On top of it all, I have a beautiful wife, who is everything I could want, and with all that I have dealt with in life, I learned you should hold on to something good when you get it. Besides, I try to stick to my guns, just like when I first became a police officer. My philosophy is still the same: If we weren't all that before, why should we be like that now? I need people in my corner who have been with me through thick and thin. Anybody can jump on the boat when the sailing is good.

16-Apr-2014

The Tale of Two Lives

MY LIFE IS TRULY THE TALE OF two lives; there is my life before becoming a cop and my life after becoming a cop. Prior to becoming a cop, my life was crazy: always broke, never really living, always in survival mode, always behind the eight ball. Definitely no support system. It was only by the mercy of Allah that I made it through those times. When your money is short, even your own mama and daddy aren't willing to invest but so much time in you. It's just the way most people are; it's all about your social status, your money, who you are. If you aren't considered somebody of importance or someone with a little clout in the hood, most people just look at you like another insignificant nigga. Sounds like hard talk, but that's the way it is. Some of the first things niggas from the Bricks say about a dude is "Yeah, he's that dude who drive this" or "He be dressin' like that" or "He work for such-and-such," and of course, they say, "Yo, that nigga making paper; he out there getting it in" (hustlin' those drugs). It's all about image in the hood. When you're known on the streets, you're having so many people who are suddenly your long-lost cousins, and all of a sudden, when they hear your name mentioned or they see you, they'll say, "That's my man."

Especially the ladies in the Bricks; they love a man with status in the hood. That's probably why so many of those hood hookers, as I call them, want to be with either a drug dealer or a cop. Logic in the hood is not always rational, and it's not easily explained. What is right by most standards is usually wrong in the hood. In the Bricks, you will find people both old and young, glorified drug dealers who once terrified neighborhoods and most certainly destroyed families with all of the drugs they sold on the block.

There is one drug dealer in particular who comes to mind; his name is Abdul Salaam Prachard, the man who I think is single-handedly responsible for the devastation of that crack period, which held Newark in a chokehold for the better part of the eighties. I can now see the full effects of that time on the young people we have out here today. So many of these kids are diagnosed with behavior and mental health problems, and many have attention deficit disorder. I know there will be those who want to be the devil's advocate and ask where my PhD is, what gives me the knowledge to say all of this about crack cocaine? I say to the naysayers, all it takes is a little common sense and research into the subject. Look at the ratio of kids being diagnosed with these health issues prior to the crack era and the ratio after the crack era.

But in spite of all of this, and in spite of most of us in the Bricks having lost a family member to crack, there's a lot of people who still plead this man's case; in fact, there was a rumor that some group had gotten together a petition to get him freed from prison. Are you fucking kidding me? Like I said, this ghetto logic is crazy. That's especially why after becoming a cop, even with the increase in my hood status, I am sad to say I'm very untrusting toward my people from the Bricks. As much as I love my city on one hand, living life here has shown me you can't trust no one. I still joke sometimes that since I moved from Newark, I'm now able to get a good night's sleep. I don't sleep with one eye open any more. But am I really joking? There was a time I was even paranoid about eating at restaurants in the hood. You never know; somebody I locked up in the past could be working in the kitchen. As cops in the inner cities, we lock up so many people over our careers. We may forget their face, but they don't forget ours.

17-Apr-2014

WHEN YOU'RE POLICING IN THE CITY WHERE you grew up, you often come across people you know. Sometimes it becomes difficult, especially if you have to arrest someone who was cool with you growing up. But when duty calls, you have to do your job; it's what you took your oath to do. I remember when I signed on to work for this security firm, Security Patrol Inc. I ended up doing security at my old apartment complex, Brick Towers. I had moved from Brick Towers a few years after becoming a cop. I had to, not just because the building was going down but Brick Towers had become a haven for drug activity, and it just didn't look good for a cop to live around those conditions.

When I started my outside employment job at the Bricks, I thought it might be a little awkward at first, policing the area where I grew up. But surprisingly, most of the people in the complex were very receptive of me; they remembered me from the hood growing up, and they gave me my respect. The security company had the detail at the Bricks for several months before I started there; they had a federal contract with the housing authority, so on each shift, there were four cops, four armed guards, and four security guards. With such a heavy security presence, the open sale of drugs at Brick Towers was almost totally shut down. With that being said, the young dudes at the Bricks still showed me respect, in spite of their money flow being drastically cut.

Of course, now and then, you come across a clown who just wants to try you, no matter what. Like one day, I was assigned to the courtyard, and this dude named Dexter was there, arguing with his girlfriend. Now this goon and me had a little history when we were younger. When I worked at the car dealer, he would always ask me to borrow some money; problem was, the nigga never paid me back. Sometimes I would tell him I didn't have it to spare, and he acted like he wanted to get tough. A few times I called him out, like, "What's up, bro, you tryna rob me or what?"

Anyway, on that particular day, he was screaming and cursing his girl out in the yard, so at first, I didn't step in right away, 'cause growing up around the way, I was used to so-called boyfriends and girlfriends yelling and arguing. But then Dexter stepped over the line; he told his lady that he was gonna beat her ass. Sorry, dog, you are not gonna threaten a woman in front of me; it's just not happening. I confronted him about this and told him to step off before he made me have to do my job. This fool started getting tough with me; bad decision, dog. I quickly put out his fire with a two-piece combination to the chin and a little pepper spray. He had the rest of the night in jail to think about it. Aside from a few instances, most of the cats around the way would just see me and say, "That's Hakim; let him get that."

One thing I can say about myself, and not to toot my own horn, but I have always tried to be fair to everyone on the streets. I've always tried to treat people like I would like to be treated. I also noticed from working my old building how many of the people I grew up with really haven't grown up at all; some people are just content to live under the same circumstances and conditions, no matter what. It's one thing to go through ups and downs in life; that's part of life, but there are many of us in the hood who are just content living from one generation to another on welfare. They just don't try to better themselves in any way. I saw quite a few men and women who were addicted to drugs ten or fifteen years ago, and they're still on the shit.

What's kills me is how some of us are so quick to say how the system or white people are keeping them down. Sometimes, if you wanna see who's keeping you down, just look in the mirror. At the end of the day, however, I have nothing but love for my Brick Towers family; I would take a bullet for some of them because no matter what our differences may have been growing up, there is a certain bond you get from your brothers and sisters in the hood when you grow up under poverty. It's like a family who sometimes fight amongst each other, but let some outsider mess with somebody in the family and see how quick they come together.

18-Apr-2014

School Days

I CAN STILL REMEMBER MY FIRST DAY of kindergarten at Quitman Street School. My parents were afraid that I would be shy, and they thought I would have trouble adapting, considering I had never spent too much time away from them, but to their surprise, I blended in nicely with the other kids. I loved my teacher; her name was Mrs. Sikes. She gave me such a warm greeting, and she was a very caring and friendly teacher. She had such a way about her that you always felt comfortable and relaxed; even though I was very young, I still remember how she had a way of instilling confidence in the kids. She had such a motivational persona about her (something I wish more teachers would have had during my time; most of the teachers I remember from my school days usually tried to rule the classroom with fear). Another thing I loved about Mrs. Sikes was that she inspired us to be creative; we were always doing class projects and not just sticking with the same boring school curriculum.

I had two good friends in kindergarten, my boy Henry and Moses. We were very close, even after school; sometimes, my parents would take us all to the park, and we would play. Those were the days just being a kid: no worries, no bills, and all-day energy. That all changed the day my parents told me what happened to my big bro, Greg Austin. It seemed like that event set off a chain reaction in my life. It was almost like no matter how well things would seem to be going during any given year, I could always count on some catastrophe to come along whenever things seemed good.

Then again, maybe most people experience these moments in life; what do they say? Into each life some rain must fall. Damn, other people do have problems, but with life in the hood, it seems like all your problems are traumatic and life altering. After kindergarten, I started St. Mary's Elementary School on MLK Blvd. It was a Catholic school, so they enforced strict discipline right from the start. It wasn't hard for me; I was a quiet, reserved kid, so I didn't make much noise in school in the first place, plus, unlike many of today's kids, I was afraid of my parents, so I didn't want any problems. Things started off well for me at St Mary's. I got along very well with most of my teachers; they took a liking to me, for some reason. I guess it was the pretty hazel eyes and all (lol).

One of the few teachers I didn't really like or get along with was my second-grade teacher, Mrs. Paula Panansky; she was one of those teachers who like to rule her classroom with fear. I just don't believe you get the most out of a child (or anyone for that matter) by making them afraid of you. I'm all in favor of teaching discipline, but no child should be in fear when going to school. I still managed to do well academically in her class; combine that with the fact that I wasn't a troublemaker from the get-go, so she didn't bother me much.

Most of my years at St. Mary's, I stayed on the honor roll, at least until seventh grade, that is. In seventh grade, we had this nun named Sister Joan; she was one mean bitch (well, at the time I thought she was). A nigga couldn't get a break in her class. She showed me what it would be like to deal with an annoying boss on a job; she was on my back constantly, sometimes over the smallest shit. I could understand this if I was a troublemaker, but in seventh grade, I was still a quiet, unassuming type of kid. I was so glad to get out of seventh grade; it was like being in prison with that chick. I think the whole nun thing and not getting no dick had that bitch trippin'. Eighth grade was pretty good for me; we had a wonderful teacher, Sister Judith. She had a strong personality, but she was very fair and understanding. By then, however, I couldn't wait to get out of St. Mary's. You know how it is; by now, I was a young teenager, and the whole discipline thing was starting to wear thin. I swear to God, when I graduated from there, I felt like I had just gotten released from prison. I couldn't wait to start high school. I was looking forward to a new start, to put the past behind me and move on. Going to St. Mary's was a trip. We even had a principal, a nun named Sister Nancy, who looked just like a dude. The kids used to call her Frankie (lol).

19-Apr-2014

Bloomfield Tech Days

STARTING HIGH SCHOOL WAS A NEW BEGINNING for me; it was also like a pet fish being thrown into the ocean. Good old Essex County Vocational (aka Bloomfield Tech). Now when you first think of a high school in Bloomfield, New Jersey, you think of the city of Bloomfield itself: a small suburban township, a relatively quiet little town with a low crime rate, a nice little college campus, and a well-manicured shopping center. So naturally when I thought of a high school in Bloomfield, I thought it would be a quiet, peaceful little school. Man, was I in for a surprise. From day one, I could tell high school was gonna be an adventure after the orientation speech from the principal, Mr. Alexander Trentaro (I'll never forget him; he was a rather tall, fat Italian man with crooked feet).

Some of the guys in my freshman class and I were on our way to homeroom when we heard a loud scream coming from the center of the building. We would have gone the other way, but we had to go that way to get to our homeroom. When we got to the center of the building, we saw what the reason was. I saw a line of upperclassmen on both sides of the hall, and the screams were coming from freshmen who had to walk through the line to get to their classes. This was called a Mumfrey line; you had to cover up and walk through the line while the people in the line tried to sneak in body punches. Now imagine a kid like me, who was used to the discipline of Catholic school, where the nuns and the priest were on you like a cheap suit, and now I was in a situation like this. I didn't see a teacher or a school guard in sight. At that point, I was wishing I was back at my old prison, St. Mary's. Thankfully, when it was my time to have to go through the Mumfrey line, a teacher finally appeared and broke up the line. Because I was kind of big for my age, I was often tested my freshman year, mainly by older students. Luckily, I had started my boxing training, so I could hold my own pretty well, especially when some the guys wanted to punch me hard to the body.

Once I got accustomed to high school, I quickly learned the clannish culture of Bloomfield Tech. You quickly learned where you fit in. I learned which groups to hang with and which groups not to fuck with. The Puerto Ricans had their own group; they called themselves the High City Swingers (HCS). They ran a lot of shit around the school; many of them were in the auto shop classes. Then you had the electric shop classes, the carpentry shop boys, and the plumbing shop crew. I eventually landed in plumbing shop as my major. There were a few more shop classes, but those were the top shops, so to speak.

For a technical high school, Bloomfield Tech had its share of attractive females. Most of them were upper class, so they weren't tryna mess with no freshmen. When my second year came around, I became more popular in the school, but my grades began to drop off. I think those puberty hormones were really starting to kick in, and my mind was consumed with trying to be with the in crowd and chasing girls. Plus, I guess it's a male thing, but when guys are young and full of testosterone, they just have to show the world how tough they are, so of course, from time to time, I still had to check a couple of people.

One fight I had my sophomore year that stands out was with this Puerto Rican kid they called Mace. It all started after we both wanted to get with this girl named Judy Gonzales; they used to call her Judy Booty, so as you can imagine, she had an ass for days, combined that with pretty olive skin and long dark hair, and you could see why we were beefin' over her. So one day, Mace starts telling everybody how he gonna fuck me up after school. So the type of dude I am, I'm not gonna let a threat go unchallenged, so I confronted him in the lunch room. I had been working on my right cross the whole weekend before the confrontation, and I put it to good work in the lunch room in front of a full house. After that fight, my school cred went up even more.

But as I stated earlier, my grades did suffer some sophomore year, and at the end of the year, I had to go to summer school for the first and only time in my life. Junior year, I got back on point with my grades and so forth. I was now an upperclassman at Tech, and I usually got the respect that went along with that. I also had my first teacher crush in my junior year. I had a health teacher named Christina De Benedetto; she had blonde curly hair and an ultra thick body, with great legs. I really had to catch myself in class because from time to time, I would find myself staring at her instead of looking at the blackboard and my lessons. But overall, she inspired me to get good grades in her class because I didn't want to look like a dummy in front of my sweetheart (lol).

To get off the high school subject for a minute, life can go in many directions, and often it's just a matter of being patient and things will come. A perfect example of that was my crush on Mrs. De Benadetto. In high school, of course, she wouldn't give me any play at all; you can understand why, being I was a student and all (even though nowadays, you hear a lot about teacher-student relationships, lol). But in my case, fast-forward eleven years after I graduated high school, eight years after I became a cop. I just happened to see Mrs. D. in Hobby's Restaurant on Brandford Place in Newark. I was taking a lunch break, and she was getting a sandwich; she told me that she was now working for the board of education on Cedar Street in Newark. Mrs. D. was still looking good; she was eleven years older than me, so at the time, I was twenty-eight and she was thirty-nine, so she was still a young woman. I got her phone number, and after speaking to her over the phone a few times, we went out to dinner one evening.

Over dinner, I expressed to her how attracted I was to her in school, and to my surprise, she told me she was attracted to me as well; she said how she was always looking at my beautiful eyes. After dinner, we reached a mutual agreement on what our future friendship would consist of: lots of wild sex. Me and Mrs. D. got it on for a good year; we fucked hard and heavy. I never knew how much of a freak she was. I can still remember the first time I hit it from the back; she bent over and wow, the big white ass hunched up on the bed and me going in and out. I still get goose bumps just thinking about it. We did it in the bed, the car, the house, and late at night in the park. See, high school crushes can turn out to be wonderful experiences.

Now back on the subject of high school. My senior year in high school was an up-and-down year. I did well in school, but my life after school was hectic; my father lost his job, and some days, we did not know where our next meal was coming from. At times, my father behaved like a pure ass; there was always an argument in the house, usually over money with him and my mother, and when you're a young adult trying to get your life started, just that in and of itself can be challenging, so who the hell needs to deal with a lot of internal bullshit in your life? All of this and more is why on his last few months on this earth, I refused to go visit him, even though he was dying. I know it sounds hard, but life makes you hard. I now try to put that part of the past behind me, but I'll be the first one to tell you I'm far from perfect. I only ask God to please help me to become a better man when it comes to forgiveness.

When I graduated high school, I was filled with emotions: happiness to be an adult, fear of the unknown, and apprehension because now I had to go out and deal with the real world. My main emotion was excitement because now my destiny was in my hands. My parents were advocates for Catholic school, and they had initially hoped I would go to Catholic high school like St. Benedict's or Seton Hall, but as people make plans, God has his own plans, and for my future job as a police officer, I was better off going to Bloomfield Tech. Once I became a cop, I saw that a lot of my schoolmates from Bloomfield Tech were now cops. It almost seemed like half of Newark PD went to Tech.

20-Apr-2014

As a writer, I focus on trying to inspire people to reach higher. I wanna show them how I was able to escape my surroundings with a pen and paper. Even during my childhood, I was able to escape my turbulent and troubled surroundings by getting into books and by writing. There was a period in my career as a cop where I concentrated just on cop shit, things like working part time, whoring around with the ladies (I know a lot of cops will be mad at me but what they say about most cops is true: they are whores), partyin' hard when the opportunities presented themselves. My whole life revolved around being a cop, and while a job (and in this case a career) is a great thing to put your all-and-all into, and it should be an important part of your life, the key phrase in that statement is "part of your life."

My job as a cop was my profession; it didn't define me as a person. It's great to be known for doing one thing very well, but I'm the type who likes to do a few things well. I like to evolve as a person and reinvent myself every so often. As a cop, I saw how easy it could be to lose that job; that's why I continued my education while on the force. You never know when something could go wrong, so I tried not to put all my eggs into one basket. I saw quite a few people who came on the job with me who didn't make it to the finish line. Some were killed on the job, some died from natural causes, and others just lost their jobs for one reason or another. I wanted to make sure I had backup, just in case something went wrong. Hell, I'm just that kind of person. I like to shoot for the stars. I wanted, with the help of God the almighty, to live my life to the fullest. I refuse to limit myself. I wanted to be more than just a retired cop who goes out and gets a security job after he retires (not that there's anything wrong with that, but I want the next chapter in my life to be different from the previous one). I love writing, and if my work can help me to inspire others to be the best they can be, then I will know that I have achieved the excellence that I strive for.

Every soul has its own individual and unique calling; not everyone wants to shoot for the stars. There are those who are perfectly happy with the same old mundane routines; there are plenty of folks who like to take the safe and secure road without taking chances in life. They just never go against the grain, and that's fine; you can only be who you are. The problem I have with some people is when they try to change you into what they want you to be. I find it hilarious how some people still think to this day that they can live their life through someone else.

No, it just simply doesn't work like that; you can only live your life to the best of your ability. That is one of the biggest problems that has always existed between me and my father, and that's why even to the day he died, we were never that close. I got the impression from day one he was trying to live through me; he wanted to make up for all of his failures through me. I guess that's why he gave me his name and made me a junior. That's why one of the first things I had to do for myself for my sanity was to legally change my name. No one has the right to try and live through someone else, just as you can never really be successful trying to live off of someone else's coat tails. If you have a successful friend or family member, trying to live off of their accomplishments will only hold you back from being all you can be.

That's what I love about writing or any other form of art. I'm able to express myself in my own individual way. I've always hated having constrictions. I guess that why I couldn't excel to my best in Catholic school; hell, let me keep it real: While I think I had a good career as a cop, I really didn't do as well as I could have; I guess it's just in my nature. I have a rebellious streak in me and hate restrictions.

That's why even with Al Islam, which is the core of my life and my whole existence, I refuse to be restricted. I try not to be complacent in this life; I keep reaching for more. I was happy with my police pension and a good job as a journalist, but I wanted more. I always wanted to write a book; Lord only knows my life has been a story in and of itself. I don't mean to toot my own horn, but I think my life could possibly become a motion picture (lol). One of my other books is about awareness in the African American communities; this book wasn't just about making money (although let's be honest, a few extra bucks is always a good thing), but this was my way of giving back to my community. Just maybe one of my books can inspire some young black brother who is dealing with some of the same problems I dealt with coming up in the hood; at one point, I was possibly on my way to jail until the good Lord above chose to take me in a different direction. If not for God's amazing grace, I would probably be serving a long sentence with my cousins in jail. That's another reason why I don't think I ever became the best cop I could have been. In this line of work, it takes a certain kind of person to really excel at that job. I've often heard it said that most cops are the type of people who were punks in school or geeks who never fit in. So now as policemen, they are mad at the world and out for revenge. Now me, myself, I may have been a bit of a geek, and I did have to deal with my share of bullies, but one thing I have never been (and never will be) is a punk. No matter how scared I may have been, I have always stood up for myself.

So I don't think I quite fit that stereotype. That's why I love this new career a little more than my old career. I'm a firm believer that sometimes, people just need a break in life; most people just need a second chance.

At the end of the day, that's what America is supposed to be about: second chances, right? Or is it that second chances only apply to certain people? How many of us as people in general usually get it right the first time anyway? I've seen so many of the people I grew up with go the wrong way in life; some were able to get themselves straight after the initial mistake and move on, while others couldn't seem to get out of the rut. I saw plenty of halfway decent guys (or at least I thought they were decent) who just couldn't get a break after getting in trouble, and it's sad because some of them are very skilled and talented guys.

One guy in particular comes to mind: my boy Jamal; here was a kid who not only had a CDL license, he also had a certificate in programming and fixing computers, but he has always had the hardest time finding a somewhat decent job. And it's not like he is the type who is constantly in trouble. He is forty-nine years old now; the last time he was arrested was when he was thirty-two. All of this stems from the charge he had at that time, a charge of drug distribution. It's not like he was a big-time dealer with major money and big cars and the like. He did his six months at the Union County Jail and thought it was all behind him. I did some research on the matter and found out that that particular charge stays on your record for up to ten years; most people with that charge have trouble finding a job afterward. Wow, how certain decisions you make in your life, how just a lucky break here and there can change your life for the better (or worse).

21-Apr-2014

Hater Nation

As you go up the ladder in life (or for that matter, even when you aspire to do well in life), you will most certainly have to deal with the haters. I know I certainly have dealt with my share of haters. They are usually low-budget, Section-Eight, nothing-happening niggas who couldn't make a pimple on a successful person's ass. It's so easy to sit back and hate on another person's blessing. My philosophy has always been this: Don't hate, go out and create your own destiny, and God willing, you will be able to duplicate that person's success—who knows; you might even rise higher and achieve more than that person.

Growing up in the heart of the Central Ward, I often encountered haters, even back when I worked at the car dealer and all I was making was four dollars an hour. All they saw was me coming back and forth wearing a blue uniform. Niggas who were just too damn lazy to get off their ass and even make an attempt to get a job. There was this one lazy fool named Tookie; he was a junkie son of a bitch who only cared about getting his next fix. I knew him from the time I was a young kid; he was cool in the beginning, but by the time I was an adult, he had become hooked on heroin. Every time he would see me come in from work, he would ask me if he could borrow a few dollars. It finally took me coming close to blows with that piece of shit to get him to stop asking me for money. Oh well, Tookie eventually died a couple of years later from AIDS, so it was probably better I didn't fight him anyway. If it wasn't the begging bitches you had to watch out for, you had to look out for the stickup kids. Now, if you were to ask me, if you were a real criminal, why would you want to go after a working man who lives in the ghetto, just like you? Really.

I'll never forget this one incident. I had just gotten off of work and was walking down MLK Blvd. when this grimey ass nigga named Nafee came up to me. I knew of him from the area but never fucked with him; he just wasn't my cup of tea. Anyway, this fool came up to me that day and asked for a handout, but in the same sentence, he tells me how he has one of his fellas positioned on this corner and another one over here and one over there and how they were waiting to jump me if I didn't give him what he wanted. My initial response to him was to go to hell. But then as usual, the numbers game was a factor in the hood. I saw four niggas walking my way with their hands in their pockets, so I just took twenty dollars out of my pocket and threw it on the ground in front of him. I said, "Fuck, if this punk-ass twenty means that much to you, take it." You can only imagine that once I became a cop that fool was on my radar. Every time I saw that clown after becoming a cop, he would start walking at hyperspeed to get out of my sight. I was just waiting patiently for old boy to fuck up so I could lock up his punk ass.

The situation never materialized. Nafee was eventually killed a little while later, probably by someone he had tried to rob before. You know what they say: God don't like ugly, and what goes around, comes around. Once I became a cop, the hate really started. I've noticed how much people of all shapes and kinds dislike authority. I really can't talk myself because prior to becoming a cop, I didn't like cops much myself, and to this day, I'm still not too fond of a lot of them. When it comes to haters, cops can be some of the biggest haters around. I've seen these new age officers stab each other in the back on many occasions, and it's usually over some form of jealousy. Guys become jealous because this person has a nice assignment and they don't. Cops are quick to say, "Why does he [or she] have that assignment? I got more time on the job than they got. That person has never worked that hard; the only reason they have that position is because they have political connections."

Please stop the hate; they know if they could pull the same strings, they would in a heartbeat. I know I would, and I wouldn't give a damn who liked it and who didn't. Now as a journalist/writer, I know there's probably plenty of hate out there for me. I can guarantee it. Where at one time all the hate bothered me, now I love it. As I've stated several times before, when I create controversy, that puts more dollars in my pockets. So haters, please keep hating. My future plans include making millions and millions off my haters. I really have to watch my back to some degree now because my haters are some very powerful people; some are major players in the drug trade. They are powerful political figures, heads of state, and even corrupt cops. Yes, I said it: corrupt cops. My feelings are that if you disrespect the badge, you deserve what you get.

As a journalist, some of my most disturbing stories have been abroad, where I've done stories on the way women are treated in some of these other countries. We take a lot of things for granted here in America. The things you will see in these other countries are heart wrenching. Some of these countries in northern African and certain parts of Asia are still treating women like it is the Dark Ages; in some of these countries, women are forced into prostitution and treated as modern-day slaves. I know some will say that this also goes on in this country, and that's true, but in this country, once government officials or someone with authority finds out about this shit, believe me—something will be done. Some of these other countries act like this is a normal way of life. I feel good when I'm able to bring light to some of these horrendous situations. I guess growing up around all of the injustice that I saw in my youth made me sort of a champion for justice. I have always hated bullies of any kind, whether they're street bullies, corrupt politicians, or police officers. I can't stand to see the weak being exploited, so if I can help someone who's being taken advantage of, I'm all in.

22-Apr-2014

Jones and Massenburg Family Reunions

SOME OF THE BEST MOMENTS OF MY life have come at family reunions. I was so blessed to finally meet my family members, even if it was later in life. I never knew I had so much family out there, all over the country. It's such a surreal moment when everyone comes together for a festive and joyous occasion. I have family members in all walks of life. Some are celebrities, some are lawyers, many just everyday working people. I met one cousin who is big in the music industry, but he was on that bourgeoisie shit; you know the type, thought he was better than everybody, the type who think everybody lookin' for a hand-out. I had to make it clear to one of his assistants (yeah, this nigga came to a family reunion with an entourage) I make my own money, and while I didn't have his money, I'm good. I even had a good time with the thug-out version of the family.

At a family reunion, it shouldn't matter who you are or what you do; it's about family getting to know family. And as far as the thugs in the family go, some of these young men I met were very bright and engaging; if only their lives could have taken another direction. A short time after one of the reunions, a couple of young men, Tyvon and Quadeer, were arrested for gun running and drugs; they were convicted and sentenced to thirty years in federal prison under RICO charges. They were the alleged heads of one of the most notorious street gangs on the East Coast. It's such a shame; from time to time, I will look online and see some of their writings from prison, and I say to myself, *These kids are so talented and intelligent.*

Then again, I've seen many cats who were as dumb as a rock when they first went to jail but after doing a bit, they seemed like scholars when they came home. I guess there's not much else to do in jail but read, study, and work out. I just wish somehow, some way, my little cousins could have gotten a second chance to get it right. But at the end of the day, we all must answer for our sins. Another thing I've noticed at my reunions is that I have some extremely attractive female cousins. I'm glad that I'm getting to know who they are; I don't need another incident to happen like the one with my niece.

One of my many regrets in this life is that none of my grandmothers are here to see my success. Nothing against my grandfathers, but unfortunately, they were both gone before I was born, so I never got to know them at all. I especially loved when the reunions were held in North Carolina.

Good old North Cacalaca is like the home base for the Joneses and the Massenburgs. Over time, the family tree branched out to many other names like the Lynches, Evanses, Moores, Scotts, and Briggs, to name a few. This family tree spreads through various parts of the country, and I've been fortunate to become close to many family members, so when I have to travel with my job or when I want to take a vacation in the States, I usually have a family member somewhere close, so it saves me money on hotels (lol).

One of the most important things I can do now as a father is keep my son in touch with his family. I'm determined not to repeat the mistakes of my old man. I'll teach my son the importance of family because when it's all said and done, that's all you have. Outside of family and a few close friends, everyone else is a stranger. Not to sound like an activist or anything, but I believe certain people don't want African Americans to ever become close with our family ties; I'm a firm believer in the saying "A people divided can never be united." And the first step in uniting a people is to unite the family structure. I also believe this to be one of the biggest reasons for the spread of gangs in the urban hoods. A lot of this comes from young people not having a strong family foundation. Most people in general have a sense of wanting to belong to something, some group, some organization. Most want the security of knowing someone has your back, that you can count on someone. That's where the family foundation comes in. If you know and become close to your family, you can satisfy that need to belong to something because with strong family ties, you will belong to something special.

I gotta keep it real; the men in my family sure as hell put a lot of work in with the ladies. These niggas were some rolling stones for real. My grandfather had five kids from his first wife; this was before he married my grandmother. Then once he married my grandmother, he had nine kids with her. My second cousin Hassan's father was the Don Juan of the family; he had twenty-three kids. And then I met other cousins with five, six, and seven kids. I'm like, "Wow, it took me until I was in my forties before I had one child, and while most of these cats are older than me, a few are younger than me." Two in particular are in their early thirties and have five kids. My cousin Hassan isn't quite up there with his pops, but he has eight of his own. I suppose I have a lot of catching up to do; you know, gotta keep up the family name (lol). Naw, that's all right, I'm good; just the way I am. Nothing against having a big family, but at my age, now is not the time. Even back in my player days, I never wanted to have too big of a family, even when I got married. I'm glad my other cousins didn't see things the way I did; if they did, we would have an even bigger family than we have.

23-Apr-2014

Black and Green

As a nation, we have grown so much, but there is still much growing that needs to be done. I hear people say that it's no longer about the color of your skin, it's all about the color green (money). And for a while, I thought that myself, but the ugly head of racism is still (and I guess it will forever be) a very relevant factor in this world. Even as I am now part of the so-called 1 percent, I still have times where I feel I'm discriminated against because of the color of my skin. And don't get me wrong, discrimination doesn't just come from people of a different race. Often, your own people discriminate against you. Some may ask how that is possible. I'll give you an example of what I mean: When I first came on the job as a cop, I was so young and looked even younger. There were plenty of times when I would simply be doing my job, and my own people would give me such a hard time. I was called everything from a sellout to an Uncle Tom. But you let a white officer come along and give them the same instruction, and they would go along with it with no problems.

When I worked at the car dealer prior to being a police officer, I was one of only three blacks there out of about thirty guys. The rest were all white. The dealer and the corporation itself were owned by people from Hong Kong, so many of the office workers were Asian. As a whole, I was always treated pretty good, but every time the subject of race came up, I would soon see how many of them really felt. Granted, they would be careful not to say too much about blacks around me, but I could hear the way they would talk about other minorities, in particular Hispanics. I worked there around the time of Desert Storm, and being that I'm Muslim, I had to endure their remarks about Islam. Yes, of course, they would try to play it off as though it was just a Middle Eastern or Arab thing, but I got the feeling that deep down in their heart, they really had a problem with a young black man who practiced Islam, a faith that they feared and were totally ignorant of.

I really saw their true colors after another incident that took place at the dealership. There were several women who worked in the office area. There were two Hispanic girls, two blacks, and four Asians who worked the main office. There was a young lady named Jillian who worked in the front office as a sales manager. She was a white girl, very intelligent with a very sweet demeanor. Jillian and I had a good work relationship right from the door. She was very kind and easy to talk to; this was probably why most of the customers loved her (the fact that she was cute as hell could have been a factor as well). She had a pretty pale complexion with long red hair and a nice petite, shapely figure to go with it. Now here's a young lady who is just naturally a friendly, pleasant person, and I guess she liked my personality, because I try to be respectful to everyone; if you treat me right, I treat you right. It's a simple approach, but it usually works for me. So Jillian and I would often be seen talking during our spare time, and a couple of times we ate lunch together in the lunch room. All of these times were perfectly harmless and innocent. We were just two people who had a cool work relationship.

But I could see the looks we would get sometimes from the white guys who worked there. I didn't pay them much attention; I knew we weren't up to nothing, but then again, what if we were? We were two consenting adults; what's the problem? Like they say on the streets, let's keep it 100; the problem they had, they didn't like seeing a young Negro messing around with a young pretty white girl. After a while, we started to hear about little rumors that were being spread around the job about us. At first, Jillian didn't pay it any attention; in fact, she suggested that that we play it off and really make them think something was going on. But over time, the rumors got worse and worse, and I could tell it was starting to get to Jillian. Me being the type of dude I am had to confront a couple of the guys who were talking shit about us. One confrontation almost got physical with me and this guy named Dave; he was a tall, kinda geeky-looking white dude. I always thought he was an undercover klansman anyway. So after the confrontations and a meeting between all parties and the service manager, a mutual agreement was reached that the spreading of rumors would stop, and they did. But by then, I could see the toll all of the nonsense had taken on Jillian. She found another job a few months later and left the car dealer.

After becoming a cop, I encountered a little less racism from other races. That is, just every now and then, I would walk by a car driven by a white lady, and even if I was in full uniform, I could hear her lock the door when I walked by. That seemed strange to me, considering how I was sworn to uphold the law and to serve and protect, but yet I felt like I was being looked at as a criminal. I felt like yelling out to them, "I'm a young black man making $100,000 a year. I don't need to rob you." I think that would be a good topic for my next book, about the color of the skin or the color of money.

24-Apr-2014

As a child, I was afraid of the mentally ill. I looked at people with mental illness like they were cursed or like they were some type of a demon or alien; in my neighborhood, there were certain guys who had mental problems, and they were usually harassed and picked on. No wonder I could count on seeing them go off every so often. Most people around the way used the mentally ill for their amusement and recreation. What kind of sick bastard does that? People really can be cruel, especially kids.

I remember going to school and seeing kids who were a little older than me picking on this young man named Andre, who lived on Lincoln Street in the projects. They would yell and curse at him and throw rocks and bottles at him. You would often see Andre yelling at the top of his lungs and chasing them down the street. Andre wasn't a punk; he didn't back down from those niggas. I just hated to see him picked on; he was really a nice guy. He came from a very religious family, and on Sundays, he would sing in his church's choir. He just had a little mental disorder, and if he didn't take his meds, he would be a little out of character, so to speak. When I would see him being picked on, I would wish I could do something about it. I had no idea that several years down the line, I would have the power to do something about it.

When I went to Saint Mary's, I remember there was a janitor named Nathan Wheeler. Nate was a big, strong, burly man, warm and pleasant in demeanor. If you spent a little time around him, you could see he was a little off board. Nate was a very hard-working brother, just trying to make a living and take care of his family. He worked for St. Benedict's High School, which was connected to St.

Mary's. I would see some of the students at Benedict's making fun of Nate; they would throw things at him when he wasn't looking. The boys were taking hell of a chance; Nate was strong as an ox, and if he ever got his hands on them, they would regret it.

In fact, there were several instances where Nate did have a conflict with these kids. For years, while I attended St. Mary's, I watched these kids harass that man, and it began to eat me up inside, until one day, I couldn't take it anymore. It was the day after my eighth-grade graduation. St. Mary's still had a few more days of school left, so I decided to visit my old school. While I was there, I saw some of the freshmen from Benedict's fucking with my man Nate. Finally, Nate had had enough; he pushed one of those little bastards, and the other three punk asses decided to jump on Nate. At first, I was hesitant to jump in, but I said to myself, *Fuck it, I don't go to school here no more, and I'm not going to Benedict's for high school.*

So I jumped in, and the fight ensued; it was me and Nate against the four of them in the locker room. The fight was eventually broken up by Mr. Darnel Brown, who was in charge of student affairs. After talking to witnesses and all the individuals involved, the staff at Benedict's cleared Nate of any wrongdoing, and those four kids were punished for starting the confrontation. I didn't see Nate for about ten years after that incident; he had retired from Benedict's but still remembered me. I was a cop by then, and when he saw me in uniform, he said he was so proud of me. He said he thought I would be a good cop.

He said how even after that incident we had with those kids, he still had problems with some of the other students. The last one prompted his retirement. He said that incident put him and a couple of students in the hospital with injuries. Luckily, there was another student who stood up for Nate; he helped Nate during the fight and testified for him in front of the board. The young man told the priest how the kids had picked on Nate so bad that if he had been a member of his family, he would have come back to that school with a gun and shot all of them.

There was another young man with mental health issues who lived in my building; his name was George Pope, and people in the hood called him Crazy George. Now I have to tell you, I was afraid of this dude; he would just be walking down the street and just snap off for no reason. This nigga was really crazy for real. Every six months, the police and EMS would come and take George away for a few months; he would come back and act normal for a few months, and then he'd start acting a fool again. I'll never forget, it was a muggy summer day, and everyone was out in the courtyard when we saw a TV come flying from the fourteenth floor and make a loud splat on the front lawn. George had thrown the TV from his window.

This time, he was taken away and stayed in a mental hospital for a long while. He eventually came home and started up again; this time, however, the ending was tragic. George jumped from his fourteenth-floor window and killed himself. When his body was being taken from the front lawn, some people from the building began to applaud. I know that seems sick, but while I never wish death on anyone, I can't say his death didn't make me feel relieved to some extent; that was one potential threat taken away from the area. As an adult and especially after being a cop, I no longer fear the mentally ill. As a cop, I've dealt with many of them, and now I realize this is an illness like any sickness, and these unfortunate souls need your help.

25-Apr-2014

The World's Oldest Profession

IT'S BEEN SAID THAT PROSTITUTION IS THE world's oldest profession, and I believe it. You see it every day, all day, in every race, culture, and community. To me, prostitution can be a housewife who gives her husband a little something extra in the bedroom one morning so she can get an extra hundred or two to go shopping, or an attractive young women in the corporate world who's willing to sell her ass to climb the ladder. And believe me, I don't discriminate how about some of these sorry-ass dudes out here who are willing to find a nice cougar and dick her down lovely so that she can take care of him. Then you have the high-priced hoes who sell pussy on the Internet, in cat houses (where prostitution is legal, of course), in go-go bars, and those who do the call girl thing. Then the last but most definitely not least: the common everyday street-walker who works the block.

It's all about using that thang to make some money; whether it's their full-time way of making ends meet or their part-time money maker, those who play in this age-old profession know that no matter how hard times are or how fucked up the economy is, there's always money to be made out here. No money no honey, ain't nothing going on but the rent, you gotta pay the cost to be the boss. All of these timeless sayings let you know you gotta come right to get that kitty cat. I learned many years ago in the hood, logic is a little different when it comes to sex. Please don't misunderstand me; like I said a little while ago, sex is used as a tool by women of all races to get what they want to some extent, but in the urban hoods, the sisters go a little extra with this shit. They know they have the ultra phat asses and the bodies, so believe me, they use it to the utmost to get what they want. Especially the Section Eight hood boogers. They can't wait till the warm weather so they can put on their daisy dukes and the minis so they can attract more customers (or victims as I like to call them).

I once saw a young cat, he looked like he was in high school, and he trying to kick it to a young high school girl; he asked her if he could give her his autograph she said yeah, as long as it's on a hundred dollar bill. I think as men in general, if we could only get back just half the money we spend on pussy in a lifetime, we would be able to retire years ahead of schedule. I often wonder why prostitution is legal in some states but not others (or, even better, why is it illegal anyway since it is the world's oldest profession and all). I don't knock nobody's hustle; my only problems with most street prostitutes is if you're the one out there taking all the risk and you're the one doing all the fuckin' and the suckin', then why do you go and give most of your money to some pimp? That's like a dumb nigga who's out there working hard as hell doing doubles every day or working two jobs and then at the end of the week, he gives all his money to some bitch.

The other problem I have with street walkers is that the majority of them are selling their ass for their next fix. Hey, if you're tricking so you can feed your kids, I'm not mad at you; unfortunately, though, the drugs are pimping these hoes. I've seen some men leave their wives and families for a prostitute. Brother who were so-called players used to say pimping ain't easy; only problem is most of these niggas ain't pimps or players: Most of them are tricks. Cats can talk all the shit they want nowadays; these chicks want paper unless they have very low self-esteem or are cougars looking for some young dick. Not trying to brag or anything like that, but over the years, I've had women tell me I'm well-endowed down there, and they said my sex game is solid, but even with all that being said, no matter how much I had them moaning and groaning or climbing the walls, I haven't met many bitches who weren't looking for a little change after we finished.

It's been said you can't turn a hoe into a housewife. I'm not too sure about that; a reformed hoe might in fact make a wonderful wife. Hoes in fact help keep some marriages together. You will probably wonder how that is. Let me tell you, I know plenty of married men who have a goomah (code name for a side piece or hoe on the low), and they're quick to tell you that their side hoe keeps balance in their married life. They tell me that smart fellas marry women who are loyal, dependable, with good morals and an overall good head on her. But they still need that sexy, freaky bitch on the side to satisfy their sexual needs.

With all of that being said, whether it's your wife or your side piece, you still got pay something for that pussy. I told you before about that freak I used to fuck with, Sasha; man, I remember times I'd be slamming her ass so good from the back she would squirt halfway across the room when she would cum, but the bitch still wanted a few dollars afterward. I should have tried selling dick on the side after the way I used to fuck these hoes; they should have been the one paying me. I'm glad I'm now with the woman of my dreams; no need for a goomah. My baby is sexy as hell and all that I need. Besides, at this point, it's cheaper to keep her. Plus side chicks cost too much. I now have a family to spend my money on. I'm a firm believer that men and women should try to get all of the freak shit out of their life before they get married.

26-Apr-2014

ONE OF MY STRONGEST PERSONALITY TRAITS IS that I've made it a point that no matter what, I never forget where I came from. Allah has blessed me to be in a good place in my life for the better part of the last twenty-eight years. But I will always try to remain humble and thankful for all that is given to me. I know life can go from sugar to shit in a heartbeat. I still remember making grilled cheese sandwiches with that government cheese. There were nights after my father lost his job at Pabst when we had spam for our meat at dinnertime. This is why if the good Lord blesses me with something good, I try to cherish it. As a police officer, I respected the badge and all that went with it. I said right from the beginning I wasn't going to be a dirty cop. I had worked too hard to get the position. I also promised to never forget my people and the struggles in the hood.

Now let me clarify that statement. Of course, I'm going to uphold the law. I took an oath to uphold it, and I take my promises seriously. But I don't believe in going out of my way to stress certain minor aspects of the law. I mean, of course I would use discretion on certain offenses, such as parking at a funeral or wedding. Some cops like to enforce every little thing. I'm not knocking them for that; in fact, in my first five years, I was a beast out there. Over time, I grew as a man and a cop. Sometimes (no, all of the time), cops should get to know their community and their surroundings. Not everybody in the hood who dresses a certain way or who wears his hair a certain way is a criminal. I grew to understand how sometimes, you can cause a great deal of damage to a person's life by putting even a minor charge on them.

One day while I was patrolling the area of Raymond Blvd. and Penn Station, I pulled over a young lady for driving while on the cellphone; she apologized for the violation and informed me that she was about to take the exam to pass the bar, and even a ticket on her record could cause her a great deal of difficulty. I knew quite a few cops who would have said, "Screw her, that's her problem," and they would have given her the ticket. God almighty tells us that blessed are the merciful, and I know I've done my share out here, so I need mercy shown to me. What would it hurt for me to show mercy to someone else? Besides, here's a young, intelligent woman with her whole life ahead of her, so why hurt the girl?

Now that I'm retired and even more financially sound in my next career, I try to use some of my resources to help improve my old hood. I know I can't save everyone. I realized that as a cop, but even if all I do is influence two or the people in my entire lifetime, I will consider it a job well done. Every two or three here and there will add up, especially if everyone who is doing halfway decent in life takes a chance to go back and try to help and influence young kids from their old neighborhood.

I already know, however, that's not gonna happen. The average negro who's doing halfway good tends to wanna look down at those who are less fortunate than them, or they think that everybody wants a handout. Real talk: You do have quite a few people who are looking for a handout. As for me, I tell a person for the beginning, while there are times when we all need help, I'm the sort of person who's more inclined to teach you how to fish rather than go out and fish for you. A man who forgets his past and where he comes from will eventually fall from God's grace and end up back in ashes. It's a lot easier to fall than it is to rise, and you see a lot of people on the way down. It brings me back to a job I had on William Street, in the heart of downtown Newark. Well, it really wasn't my job; it was an FBI job. They had just busted a big drug dealer from the area, a kid named Darrol Bradley; now, I knew of Mr. Bradley and had heard of his alleged drug connections in the area. I patrolled the downtown district, so I was familiar with all of the players, many of whom I had arrested over the years. Many of those young men literally grew up in front of me. And like I said before, work is work. I swore to uphold the law; if anybody commits in crime in front of me, I'm gonna do my job, case closed. Now while I always heard rumors about Mr. Bradley, he never did anything in front of me, and he always gave me my respect on the street. So when the feds pick him up, it came as no great surprise to me. Anyway, on that day, I was advised by my superior to stand by with the feds while they finished their investigation of the store Mr. Bradley owned on William Street.

So as they were bringing him from the store, he noticed me standing there and said, "Peace, Officer Jones, stay cool and stay safe." So the FBI soon finished their business, and I didn't think anything more about Mr. Bradley speaking to me, until a federal officer named Carol approached me and asked, "Where do you know Darrol Bradley from?"

I said, "From the neighborhood," so she started going on and on, like she was interrogating me, so finally I got a little offended and let her know about it. She quickly tried to clean it up by saying she wasn't trying to imply anything, but she didn't, for example, have any friends who were drug dealers. I simply informed her that I was a brother who grew up in the Bricks, and she was a white girl from the suburbs, so she hadn't met some of the people I knew, nor had she seen some of the shit I've seen. When I'm right, I don't care who you are, I'm gonna stand up for myself.

27-Apr-2014

PATIENCE IS ONE OF THE MOST NECESSARY, endearing, important characteristics any individual can have. They say patience is a virtue and how correct they (whoever they are) are. Without patience, you will never accomplish much. I have to keep reminding myself every day that life is a marathon not a sprint; even the great Roman empire wasn't built in one day. Usually the better things in life take time and don't come easy. When you really look back at your life, if something came easy, it usually didn't work out or wasn't that good from the door. Growing up the way I did, it looked like everything I ever tried was a struggle; sometimes, I would get a little burned out from always having to struggle for every little thing. I believe this is the reason for my complacency for a long period of my life. I stopped going to school; for the first fifteen years of my career as a cop, I was just happy to have a career and wanted to finish it and get my pension. But deep down, I wanted more.

When I first started going to college, I had a short-range goal of finishing school in five to six years, considering that I was going to school part-time, so when things didn't go as planned, I became content to just take a safe route to the finish line. This is, of course, after I became an officer (not the finish line of life but my career as a cop). I now realize that I should have continued with school no matter how long it took. I eventually returned to school in my sixteen years on the job and took a course here and there until I finally had my degree.

Lack of patience has been my downfall on a few things in this life, especially with women. My lack of patience is the reason why it took me so long to get laid. I would get easily frustrated when things didn't go my way in a relationship and once the frustration set in, I would usually do something foolish. Prior to becoming a police officer, my emotions would often get the best of me when dealing with women (not in a violent way, of course). I did indirectly stalk a few sisters in the past. I now think back like, What in the hell was on my mind? All of that came from a lack of patience.

I became much more patient during my career in law enforcement; without patience, my career would not have lasted very long. I learned to become even more patient while I was writing my books. Writing books require time, patience, and consistency. The best novels are usually written over time. Patience is essential when you have a wife and family. That holy Koran teaches us that as a man, your women and children will be amongst your most difficult challenges. Successful people are usually patient people. When I was younger, I would look at life like this: I'm getting older; if I don't get this done by a certain time, I don't want to get too old before I do this, or Damn, life is passing me by. Having the knowledge that I have of Islam, I'm now disappointed in myself for even letting these thoughts into my mind. The Koran simply says this: to live every day as though it is the last day of your life but also live every day as though you are going to live forever. I also had to learn to be patient with the people who I care about. Because you never know when you will need somebody to be patient with you. I know for a fact the Lord above has been extremely patient with me and my foolishness. If the early bird catches the worm, then a patient man will capture the kingdom. Without patience and understanding, you alienate those around you. You can also lose out on some good opportunities. In everything you want in life, you must go after it with dogged determination; in fact, when it comes to some things, you must give it several tries before you conquer it. This is where patience comes in. I saw many of the young men and women from my hood; they started off with good intentions and big aspirations, but when things didn't go right, they went off course (usually in a bad direction).

The same can be said for those brothers when they come home from incarceration. It's not easy transitioning back into society after prison, so no matter what, you have to be patient. I saw so many brothers give up and turn back to a life of crime. As I young man, I grew impatient with my financial situation. I now think back on how I could have gotten myself killed or ended up in jail with some of the things I ended up doing. Patience can ultimately play a huge factor in which direction your life will travel.

During my investigations as a journalist, I'm often required to use extreme patience when trying to complete my stories. Even though I have deadlines to meet, patience is required when leads and interviews don't work out as initially planned. Patience is also needed on this job as it was when I was a police officer, dealing with a lot of my co-workers, if you know what I mean. I can also speak from my own experience that if I had been a little less impulsive in my younger days, I would have definitely had more money in my pockets back then. You can't rush perfection. Also, as you get older, you start wanting time and everything around to slow down just a bit. One thing for sure: You don't want to rush your life away. Patience and consistency can conquer mountains. Even when the odds are stacked against you, with patience and diligence, you will more than likely prevail; like I said before, what you put in the universe comes around eventually, and when you work hard and stay positive, good results must come your way. God the almighty promises this to you. And we all know he doesn't break promises. In all religions, patience is part of faith.

28-Apr-2014

Growing up the way I did, with all the tension and drama in my life, it was no wonder that as a young man, I suffered from anxiety. I was ignorant about anxiety and panic attacks; that subject was taboo in the hood. If you even heard of the subject, you would think of a crazy nigga going around the hood talking to himself, yelling, screaming, and acting a fool. At first when I started experiencing the symptoms of anxiety, I thought I was having a heart attack. I can recall the first episode like it was yesterday because it was one of the scariest moments of my life. I was working at the car dealer in Montclair; at the time, I was nineteen years old. I was waxing a car in the showroom when all of a sudden, I felt something in my chest fell, and I started feeling gassy had chest pains. I quickly became excited, and my heart started beating quickly. I thought it would go away, and it did, a few minutes later, so I went on with my day and finished work.

Two weeks later, while cleaning an area in the service department, I started to experience the same symptoms again. I immediately started to think something was seriously wrong with me, so I advised my manager what was going on and went straight to the hospital. They hooked me up to the heart monitor, did two EKGs, and did a chest x-ray; all tests were negative. Of course, I did a follow-up visit with a cardiologist, and every test I did came back okay. The medical tests were coming back negative, but I was still experiencing those symptoms on a regular basis. Now imagine: I'm nineteen years old, a young man in the prime of my life, and I'm feeling like my life is in danger, but all of these doctors are telling me I'm good to go.

Finally, while visiting my primary care physician (remember, I never really had a family doctor; I didn't go to the doctor regularly until I was grown), he asked me if something was bothering me, if anything was causing me stress. I didn't know where he was going with this line of questioning, but he soon explained his position. He told me he thought my problems may be stress related and that I may be having anxiety attacks. I advised him that my life had been nothing but stress, so it wouldn't surprise me. Before finding Islam, my only stress relievers were when I would go to the boxing gym and when I would smoke some weed every other weekend or so. Things got so fucked up; sometimes, I felt like taking my own life. The problem with that was, would I find any weed in hell? (lol)

No, real talk: The thought may have crossed my mind, like it does a lot of people, but killing myself was never an option. Even before Islam, my belief in God was always very strong. When I finally had the courage to go to a psychologist, he diagnosed me with anxiety and mild depression. I had to go for follow-up visits and was prescribed Xanax. I tried this for a little while, but my insurance didn't pay much for mental health issues, and coming out of my pocket was getting costly. Of course, I didn't get any support from my immediate family; even knowing what I was going through, my father was still looking for his rent when I got paid.

I never ask for a handout, but damn, here's a young black man who works every day, goes to school, and generally stays away from the nonsense (at least at that time), and the nigga can't work with me? When I look back with my schedule and my life at that time, no wonder I had stress in my life. The one thing that I wanted to get away from was taking the Xanax; if the problem was in my head and my emotions, I was determined to get my mind right and stabilize my condition without prescription meds. Most of these medications are very addictive, and you become dependent on them for most of your life. These medicines limit your ability to function in this world, and you already know how I feel about living and being all you can be. So thank God I didn't stay on this medication long.

After becoming a cop, I was especially thankful that I got off the medication because I wouldn't have been able to work in that profession while taking a narcotic like that. I was still experiencing those symptoms periodically, even after becoming a cop. I continued going to doctors to find out what else may have been going on because I still had chest discomfort. It wasn't until I was in my early thirties that I found out what had been causing the chest problems. It was at that time I was diagnosed with acid reflux disease (or GERD, as it's called in some circles).

As far as the anxiety and depression shit goes, I grew up black and in the heart of the ghetto, and while I'm not making excuses or looking for sympathy, life is what it is, so I work with the hand that I'm dealt. I just deal with it and keep moving forward. I try to eventually make a weakness my strength; if it doesn't kill me, it sure as hell ain't gonna stop me.

To this day, however, I must say I'm still a bit untrusting when it comes to doctors, because while I'm no medical expert in any way, shape, or form, I can't understand why it took so many years and so many doctors before one was finally able to diagnose my chest problems. I pray to Allah I'm wrong, but I don't feel that people in urban black communities get the same medical attention that they get in the suburban areas. Who knows, maybe paranoia is another symptom I'm having (lmao).

29-Apr-2014

GUN CONTROL AND GUN VIOLENCE IS A topic that is heavily on the minds of the country. I find this a little ironic; you hear so much about gun control when a damn maniac goes crazy and shoots up a school, a mall, or some crowded area in suburban America, when in the urban ghettos, gun violence has been off the chain for the better part of four decades. Anyone who attacks innocent kids, women, or the elderly is a special kind of evil in my opinion, and most of the time, the laws are too easy on these piles of horseshit. Everyone's life is important and of value, no matter what their economic situation is or where they live. I've hated violence and bullying my entire life.

Growing up in the Central Ward, I saw the damage and destruction caused by illegal guns at a young age, long before I became a cop, and after becoming a cop, the damages I saw doubled over what I had seen previously. Now, let me make it clear: While I do hate the violence that is caused by the number of illegal guns on the street, I strongly believe in our constitutional right to bear arms if you're a law-abiding citizen of this great nation of ours.

I believe the gun laws in this part of the country are too restrictive and make it harder on law-abiding citizens. I wish we had gun laws similar to those in the Southern and Western states. I wish I could have been able to lawfully carry a weapon when the fool Nafee came at me for my money. I wish that sweet, innocent, and bright young lady Valery had a lawful weapon on her and used it on that drug addict bastard before he had a chance to take her life so unjustly at the bodega so many years ago. I wish my big brother from another mother, Greg Austin, had a gun when the punk ass bastards killed him in Weequahic Park back in the seventies.

I also strongly believe our self-defense law here in New Jersey is much too restrictive. Everyone on the planet has a God-given right to defend themselves against an aggressor. New Jersey says you can defend yourself, but you first have to retreat and show that you have absolutely no other means than to defend yourself. I know laws are set up for a reason, and I know these lawmakers have way more education than the average person. I know they have more book education than me, but personally, I like the Stand Your Ground law in Georgia and Florida.

I know a lot of my brothers and sisters in the South will say how can I, as a black, be in favor of this law when some of my own people have unjustly lost their lives because of it? I say to them it's not the law that killed our people (the act was done by some unscrupulous individuals), it was the interpretation of the law that failed to give our people justice. If a person is simply walking down the street, minding his or her own business, and someone else attacks them for no reason, then that's one thing, but if you're out here looking to hurt someone or take their property unjustly, then in my opinion, you get what you get.

There will always be those bleeding hearts who will say a law like this can cause way more harm than good. I ask them, have you personally ever been the victim of a crime? I've experienced being a victim, both before becoming a cop and after. Yes, after becoming a cop; not directly, the cowards know better. But indirectly, anybody can get gotten. A few years ago, I leased an Infiniti I 35 with the high beam headlights. At the time, those lights were a hot commodity on the streets of Newark. I wish I had known this before I took a four-year lease on the car. The first year with the car was fine, but the next three years were a nightmare. My headlights were stolen eight times within that period. One time, they took my lights when I just went into a restaurant to eat breakfast. I can only imagine what would have happened if I lived in one of those states where you can shoot someone if they're on your property unlawfully, and those crooks had come on my property to get my lights.

I know, sounds like I have some anger in me from some of my past problems; well, you're God damned right I got some hostilities. Nobody likes to be a victim. Nobody should have to be a victim. There's a saying that an armed society is a polite society. I'm a believer in a lot of what the National Rifle Association (NRA) says. Tough gun laws only make it harder for honest people to get guns to protect themselves; the criminals will always get their hands on guns. They get their guns on the street, so there are no rules or regulations they have to follow. It's never gonna be hard for them to get a gun. A gun can be used for good or for evil. The gun itself is never evil; it just depends on whose hands the gun is in and how it's used. Northern New Jersey was listed as the carjacking capital of the world; imagine how many carjackings you would avoid if these victims had legal weapons on them so that they could defend themselves. Remember, an armed society is a polite society.

30-Apr-2014

Breaking a Cycle of Ignorance

MY FATHER USED TO SAY THAT THE Apple doesn't fall to far from the tree. The Bible tells us that you are as your father was. Well, I can only say I was determined to be a totally different man from the one my father was. I wanted to be a better a much better man. From the beginning, anyone could see that I was nothing like my old man. My father grew up admiring his father, something that I could never say I did. I never got to know my grandfather; he died when my father was about fifteen years old, so by my estimation, he died twelve years before I was born. The only thing I ever knew of my grandfather was that he was a former military man and a sharecropper, which in my father's own words was another name for a slave. My only other knowledge of him was from the stories my father would tell me of him and stories I would hear from other family members.

My father of course had nothing but good things to say about him. He praised him as being a hard worker and told me how talented my grandfather was at other things besides farming; he was skilled with the guitar, a good mechanic, and a skilled barber. He also said that he was a dedicated family man who was well respected in the community. All of this would give a person the impression that he was a good man. Well, after all is said and done, he may have been a good dude and all. But certain stories I heard from other family members tell me something else. When I hear something of substance, it stays with me; whereas my father praised my grandfather, my father's other siblings had a different story to tell. I heard several of my aunts and uncles say that my grandfather wasn't shit, that he could barely take care of his family, that he often had affairs outside of his marriage, and that he could be very abusive toward my grandmother. You see back in those times, women really took their vows seriously (sometimes too seriously because even though you say for better or worse when you get married, no one deserves to be in an abusive relationship). My grandfather was married previously before marrying my grandmother, and that married didn't work out, so the lady he married before must have had the good sense to get out before it was too late. My mother would often say (usually when she was mad at my father) how my grandmother warned her before she married my father that my father had a lot of the same characteristics as my grandfather. My mother said Granny told her how my grandfather was a very controlling man with very peculiar ways; he was extremely fussy and had a bad temper.

My mother said Granny told her while she would never say she was glad to see anyone die, the passing of my grandfather bought a great deal of peace and calm in her life. She no longer had to worry about what type of mood he would wake up in; she didn't have to worry about an argument if the food was a little over- or under-cooked. She didn't have to worry about missing a dusty spot on a piece of furniture. My father's mother, Granny Annie, was a very strong woman; she married my grandfather at a young age, and after my grandfather's death, she raised nine kids, most of whom were still very young, by herself. Now that is a strong black women and a real example of strength and courage. Granny Annie and other sisters like her at that time should be on the cover of Essence magazine because they are the black girls who rock.

From what I saw from my father, he often exhibited the same characteristics as his father; now, I'm not going to lie on him. He had some good ways and wasn't abusive to my mother on an everyday basis, but he had his moments, especially when things didn't go his way. My father's mood swings could be difficult to deal with as well, especially when I was younger. As an adult and especially after I became a cop, he pretty much stayed his way and I stayed mine; he knew not to cross the line.

My biggest complaint with my father was that when I was growing up, he really didn't spend much time with me. To be a good father, you have to spend that good quality time with your child. This is very important when it comes to a father-son relationship. I believe this is why so many young men in urban communities lack the proper guidance and understanding on how a real man should conduct himself. My father would get on me from time to time when I was a preteen; he would say I was getting older and needed to start acting more like a young man. My question was, how can I ever learn to act like a man when there's no one around to teach me how to act like a man? I often wanted to do little things like play catch or shoot some baskets or even go to a sporting event with my father. I can count how many times we did any of those things on one hand. I now take into consideration that neither my father nor my grandfather finished high school, but I'm not giving either of them a pass on the wrong they did.

It's all about breaking a cycle of ignorance, and that's why I was determined to get my education. With a proper education, your mind opens up. You gain a better understanding of life and how to better handle what life gives you. My father and grandfather were raised a certain way, and that's all they knew; that's what they thought was right. I know what my job as a father is, and it's on me to do it. I can't dwell on the past. I just have to keep breaking that cycle.

1-May-2014

L AW ENFORCEMENT CAN BE A 24/7 JOB. When I was in the police academy, the instructors told us, "Once you become a cop, you're a cop every day, all day." I didn't buy into it at first. I said to myself, *I'll be a cop 24/7 when they put 24/7 worth of pay in my check every two weeks.* And I must say I still felt that way up until the end of my career. On the streets, people would often recognize me off duty in my regular clothes, and they would come up to me and say, "Hey, Officer, how are you doing?" or people would see me out somewhere and want to start asking me questions about police work or telling me about a legal problem they're having. My response would usually be, "Do you see a damn uniform on me today?" In other words, when I'm not working and getting paid to hear your problems, what's makes you think I want to hear this shit when I'm off?

This police shit is unlike any other job; the average person can see certain bullshit and just walk away from it. As a cop, your job is to walk toward the shit and handle it. Most cops work part-time to earn extra money. Most of us try to find side jobs that are relatively quiet, where you won't have too much drama; who wants to work harder on a side job than you work on your regular tour? While that may be the idea, it doesn't always work out that way; like I said, drama has a way of finding you when you put this uniform on.

Case in point: I was working at CC's Department Store on the corner of Broad and Market; it was 5:30 in the afternoon, and it had been a quiet day. I was anticipating getting off at seven o'clock and had a nice evening planned out already in my head (get off, get some dinner, have a few cocktails, etc.).

Then came the drama. Two innocent-looking young ladies who looked like schoolgirls approached me, and one of them said that she was robbed at gunpoint about a week ago and just saw the girl who robbed her up the street. Now imagine: I'm due to get off in a little while, and in a matter of minutes, the young lady was talking about walking down the street toward the store. I was tempted to try and squash this shit and walk the young ladies over to a cab and pay for them to go home, but duty called, and these young ladies looked pretty shaken up. So I snatched the suspect up and detained her until I spoke to robbery squad detectives, and they confirmed the robbery. So I ended up locking the girl up, and it turned out to be a good job. I found out this girl was wanted for about seven other robberies that had been committed in the area recently.

Some of your best jobs can be the ones you get off duty from the department. But nowadays it's so easy to get into trouble, both on duty and off; most officers try their best to avoid conflict off duty. As I became more experienced, I began to shy away from part-time side jobs; my preference for making extra money was working departmental overtime. As I stated before, trouble can find you, both on and off duty, but I just feel a bit more secure when I'm on city time and something might kick off, as opposed to getting involved in something off duty.

I have to admit it: On one hand, while I don't like getting tied up in a situation off duty, something inside me just hates injustice. Like when the young ladies told me what had happened, I thought back to some of the problems I had growing up, and at that moment, I knew that I had to take some kind of action, not just because it's my job but simply because it's the right thing to do. So many times coming up, I wish someone had been there for me when I needed help. Perhaps this was just life's way of giving me my redemption, by helping someone else.

I liked being able to help that young lady; later in my career, at a time when most cops become hard hearted and cynical toward (people usually after years of dealing with everybody's bullshit), I tried to stay to the reason for me becoming a cop (the other reason besides making pretty good money); as corny as it may sound, I wanted to make a difference in my community. Yeah, it sounds like a cliché, but that's who I am. You know, life shapes us all in some way; who we are, how we think, some of us are shaped for the best, and some are shaped for the worst, but either way, it shapes us. All of my hardships made me a warrior. I just ask the Lord above to continue to guide me so I can stay a warrior for that which is right. Sometimes in the past, I thought I had a just cause, but something would come along and guide me in another direction (that devil is a son of a bitch, ain't he?). I guess life and its struggles are just like police work: a twenty-four-hour job.

2-May-2014

I HAVE MENTIONED FREQUENTLY THAT I DIDN'T START getting to know many of my family on my father's side of the family until I was a grown man; with my mother's side of the family, it was the exact opposite. Every holiday for most of my life was spent with my mother's family; the same could be said for every family cookout, or just any family get-together in general. They were all spent with her side of the family. Only now and then, I guess when the moment would hit him, would my father get us together, and we'd visit the family on his side. Like I mentioned previously, right from the beginning, I started off with my mom's people. My grandmother basically took care of me until I was three, and after her death, I still spent the majority of my time around my mom's family.

Even though I was only three, my grandmother's death left a big void in my life and in my heart. That void was filled to some extent by my great-aunt, Beatrice Taylor, or Beatsie as she was so affectionately called. She was a light-complexioned black woman with gray eyes; in fact, she looked similar to my grandmother, and she had a similar mannerism to her as well, so I guess it was only natural that I would be so accepting of her. She stayed on Avon Avenue in Newark with some of my mother's cousins. I so looked forward to the times when that side of the family would have events over their house. When I think of that house, it brings back such fond memories of some wonderful times. It was a big old Victorian house that sat on the corner of Avon Avenue and Irving Turner Blvd. It was a brick house with steep steps, big windows, and a big back yard. They gave many parties and cookouts over there. Whenever you went over there, you knew you would have a good time and eat plenty of good food. Not only would we party with my blood family, my aunts, uncles, and cousins, but also our extended families like the Bryants and the Hendersons. Man, what I would give to go back to those days; if only I could find a time machine (lol).

Often when we would go over there for night parties, Beatsie would retire early and spend the rest of the evening in her room. I would always make it a point to go up and visit her a few times; we would spend hours just talking, laughing, and watching TV. Sometimes, just spending time with her was more fun than the actual party itself.

It was at that young age that I began to gain an appreciation for the more simple things in life. One night in particular, our family had a get-together over the house, and for some reason, I kept going back and forth upstairs all night; I'm mean even more than I would normally go back and forth to see Beatsie. Maybe this was Gods way of letting we spend as much time as I could with my beloved Beatsie because little did I know he would soon call on her to come join him in paradise. The very next morning after the party, my mom received a phone call: Beatsie had had a bad stroke, and she had been taken to the hospital. When we arrived at the hospital, we were met by the tragic news that Beatsie had died. I was seven at the time, and even at that ripe young age, I was starting to feel like, What the hell, am I cursed? I mean, first my grandmother, now Beatsie. Wow, this is not how it's supposed to be. It's not like this on TV or in the movies.

Luckily for me, I still had plenty of family left on my mother's side. I had my Aunts Dawn, Gail, and Marilyn; my Uncles Donald and Rosco; my cousins, the Taylors and Govans; and plenty of extended family. We had a very lively family on that side; there was always something exciting that would happen at a family gathering, and sometimes something dangerous. For example, I remember when I was nine, and my mother, my aunts and uncles, and I took a trip to South Carolina for a funeral; my mother's Uncle Buba had died. We took a Greyhound Bus to Orangeburg, South Carolina; it was a long ride, from what I remember, about sixteen hours. It was made easy by the fact that I was riding with loved ones, and we enjoyed each other's company the whole way.

After arriving in South Carolina, we stayed at my great-aunt Shug's house. We stayed for two days until the funeral. One evening, the family was sitting together in Aunt Shug's living room, talking about old times, just reminiscing about the good old days. I was just sitting there, taking it in; you learn a lot as a youngster just by sitting back and listening to older relatives talk about the way times have changed over the years, how people and the way they deal with things have changed. The evening was going pretty smooth; everybody was getting along, no problems. I just noticed that Aunt Shug had had a few drinks and was starting to get a little tipsy. A little while later, her ex-husband Paul came over, and that's when the drama started. Aunt Shug had a few more drinks, and then it was on. She and Paul had a few words, and the next thing I know, Aunt Shug went into the kitchen and came out with a shotgun. I never saw a group of black folks clear out a room so quick; my mother momentarily forgot about me, she was moving so quick (lol). Paul and my uncle took the shotgun from Aunt Shug. It wasn't loaded; Aunt Shug just did it to shake some people up, and a few minutes later, everybody was sitting down, laughing about the whole thing.

I had many wonderful moments with that side of the family; it's just a shame I lost so many of them when I was so young. My uncle Donald was a tall, handsome brother; he was quite the ladies' man. He had such an outgoing personality, and even though he did his thing with the ladies, his family always came first. He died when I was fifteen; he was only fifty when he passed. I really miss him; he was always so vibrant and full of life. Gone far too soon. My uncle Rosco was my man; he was the first one to take me to a boxing gym. Uncle Rosco, or Roc, as he was known in the hood, was the thug in the family. I still hear the stories from old-timers about the way he could fight and how he had dudes in check out here on the street. For all his faults, Rosco loved his family to death, and you know, it was ironic: Just as soon as he got his life together, started working and trying to live right, he got cancer and died. I lost him when I was twenty.

After his death, I did have a long period where there were no deaths in my immediate family (on that side, at least). Thank almighty God Allah, it would be sixteen years before he would call for another family member from that side of the family. Aunt Gail passed when I was thirty-six; she was the backbone of the family. Her death hurt me similar to the death of my grandmother. But her death also inspired me to go forward and strive to become a better person. The death of loved ones is difficult indeed, but I know as long as I'm here, there are still some things I need to handle. Over the last ten years, I've lost other family members, including my father. His death was difficult in many ways; while I have had my share of problems with him, he was my father, after all. I have learned to make peace with my father's memories. What's done is done, and you can't go forward if you keep looking behind you. I will need forgiveness myself, so how can I not forgive others?

3-May-2014

IT WAS A BRIGHT WINTER MORNING; THE year was 1990. The sun was out, nice and shiny, and the temperature was about 30 degrees. It's the middle of January, and I walked up the stairs of One Lincoln Ave. in Newark. This was my first day at the Newark Police Academy. Man, was I excited; this was a major step up for me. I was twenty-two years old, and now I had a real job, a career, something to be proud of. Don't misunderstand me; I was grateful for all of my past employment. God blessed me to a least have a legal means of employment, and that says a lot when you're a brother from the hood. Seven out of ten cats who grew up around me were either in jail or hustling for a living. But this was like the first day of the rest of my life. I knew from this day forward, if I did the right thing and kept my nose clean, I could have a certain degree of financial security the rest of my life.

The first day of the academy was all about mind games, so I just kept calm and stayed focused. The instructors all had on their game faces, even my Muslim brother, who I knew from the mosque: Detective Muhammad Abdul Salaam. I understood it was just business, just part of the game. For the next six months, it was their job to try and break you, to weed out who belonged and who didn't. There was one instructor, Detective Darnell Langston. I had met him several weeks before the academy, under somewhat rough circumstances; after I was laid off from the car dealership, I worked security at Newark Airport for about eight months. I worked with Detective Langston's girlfriend, Michelle Porter; she was a security officer who worked under me (I was a shift supervisor). Michelle was a cute little thing, and she was used to getting her way with most of the supervisors (and if you took one look at that tight little ass of hers, you could see why).

I was different, however; it was strictly business with me and her (well, at least at the beginning). I got along well with Michelle when I kept it strictly business, but then I made the cardinal mistake of getting too close to her. One night while we were both working the midnight shift, we started talking on a personal level; we then began a little harmless flirting. Well, one thing led to another, and then by the middle of the shift, we were making out in one of the empty offices. Things then began to get hot and heavy, and I'll leave the rest to your imagination.

From that point on, I lost my edge over her as a supervisor. She started coming to work late; she was late relieving other officers for their breaks, which caused them to complain to me since I was the shift supervisor. So finally I had to say something to her; she then in turn cursed me out. We had some words, of course, but I thought that was the end of it; that was until two days later, when her boyfriend, Detective Langston, showed up at the job to confront me. He invited me to his dojo for a "friendly sparring session."

Not to be outdone, I told him if he wanted to see me, he should come spar with me at Red Brick Gym. Well, we never did spar, and a few days later, me and Michelle made up and were cool again. Now fast-forward to the first day of the academy, and I see that Langston is one of the instructors. I think to myself, *I gotta deal with this asshole for the next six months; he's mad at me because I argued with his girl. I hope he don't know that I also fucked his bitch.* Langston was the hard-ass of all the instructors in the academy, and that was saying a lot. We had some rough characters training my class in the academy. The six months in the academy was rough, but at the same time, it was one of the best times of my life. In places like a military boot camp, college dorm, or police academy, you will meet people who will be your friends for the rest of your life. There's a special bond that grows between people during those kinds of settings, where most people are relatively young and just starting out in life, young men and women who are just trying to get through this obstacle and move on to a better, more prosperous life. Veteran instructors not only try to toughen you up for the streets, they also give you advice from what they saw in their years of service on how to not only survive on the streets but also how to survive the internal BS that goes on in any organization.

One piece of advice I remember hearing was this: You should always try to stay in good graces with your coworkers, mainly because we are all we have out here, and we have to back each other up, and also, things change on this job. You may treat a brother or sister officer bad for whatever reason, and you think, *The hell with them, we're all equals,* but you never know what the future holds in store. This same person could be your supervisor one day, and as they say, the ass you kick today may be the ass you kiss tomorrow. In the academy, I began to realize what I would later learn to be a fact. A few years later, when I became more experienced, I learned the majority of stress on the job came from the same sons of bitches that you worked with in the department. Working the street, for the most part, is the easiest part of the job (hard as it may be to believe).

Newark is Newark, and it's always gonna be Newark. If you grew up in this city, you should kind of know what to expect. The problem these days is with your co-workers, things like who is jealous of who, can you find a good partner or squad to work with, can you trust your fellow officers? I would hear some of the older instructors tell us about the comradery that cops had back in their day, but once I hit the streets, I realized those times had passed.

When I finished the academy, I was all pumped up, full of piss and vinegar, ready to take on the world. The weekend after I graduated the academy was (and still is to this day) the best weekend of my life. My aunt Gail had a cookout in my honor over her house, and members of my family from both sides came. It was great; everybody was together, having a good time. I felt like a star that day. It's good to feel like a celebrity a few times during your life; usually the only time people make a big deal over you is at your funeral (lol). It felt so good to have my loved ones with me that day. I just regretted the ones who had passed on and weren't there with us. Time is a son of a gun; we have to cherish the special times because they don't always stay the same. There would still be loved ones I would lose before I retired.

You know, back on the subject of the academy, one of the older instructors also told us to look around the class, that some of us would not make it to the end of our careers; some of us would get killed or get fired, and some may get injured and have to retire early. Back then, when you're young and healthy, it was hard for you to imagine this, but as you got older, you soon learned how real these words are.

4-May-2014

T HE DATE WAS JANUARY 30, 2015; IT was a cold winter morning. The sunrise was beautiful; still, it was one of those winter mornings you would love to just stay in bed with that special someone and chill until noon time. It was the type of morning when if you have unlimited sick time, you say to yourself, *I think it's time to throw a shoe today [call in sick]. It's just one of those mornings.* On this day, however, in order for me to call in sick, I would have to literally be on life support. This of all days was not going to be a sick day, and why should it? After that day, I was gonna have plenty of time on my hands because this was my last day as a police officer. As the morning unfolded, it looked a lot like my first day of the academy. Just like on my first day as a cop, I had a mixture of emotions and feelings: relief that I had finally made it, a little fear of the unknown, excitement because just like in the beginning, this was the first day of the rest of my life. You know, most if not all cops say when it gets to their retirement time that they will be running for the door, that they won't miss the job, and that was me included. Well, we lied. I know most cops won't admit it, but they will miss the job, and unless you got ice water in your veins, your last day will be emotional. My last day was a day for me to reminisce. I had to visit the first precinct where I started, down on Market in the East District. The precinct is one of the older precinct in the department; the building was old, and on several occasions, my fellow officers and I did our own renovations on it. Some people may say, "That's not your job; you're not construction workers or carpenters." We just looked at it like this is our home eight hours of the day, so why not take care of our home?

I spent the first eighteen years of my career there, so it was like a second home to me. After visiting my old precinct, I went around to visit a couple of my old walking posts. First I went to Penn Station; I had that post for four years. For four years, I walked seven at night until three in the morning. Those were not the most ideal hours, but it beat going around the clock. I loved working Penn Station; in spite of the hours, the station was always busy, and especially being that I was a very young man, I loved seeing all of those beautiful women commuting through Penn Station. You saw all kinds there: You saw the last batch of corporate ladies coming through as they were heading home. You saw the different college girls, especially around the holiday seasons. You saw the go-go girls coming back and forth from New York City and just everyday women in general.

The Hilton Hotel was right across the street, so I would often see celebrities and other influential people from time to time.

Penn Station was also beneficial to me from a professional aspect. I probably made the most arrests of my career at Penn Station, so much was going on, or let me rephrase that: going through Penn Station. From drugs to guns and a number of other illegal activities, you can find it going throughout any transportation station in the world, and Penn Station is no exception. While working at Penn became very cool with many of the NJ Transit police officers, one in particular was my man officer Dan Jordan. I mean, this guy could sniff out drugs and guns like a bloodhound. Many nights, I would meet up with him, and he would find me a drug arrest, and I was able to get three gun jobs with him as well. He really had an eye for getting good jobs; because of my work with him, I received four command citations and two FOP awards.

After saying my good-byes at Penn Station, I had to visit my old friends on Ferry Street. I worked that post for about a year and a half. The Ferry Street area is the restaurant district in Newark. Most of the upper-scale restaurants are in that area, so working that post, you can imagine I put on a few pounds (lol). I couldn't help it; restaurant owners loved my work, so they were constantly inviting me in for lunch, and they would be insulted if I didn't go in from time to time and get something. The Ferry Street/Ironbound area of

Newark is mostly Portuguese, and after spending time working down there, I learned a lot about their culture. I've always enjoyed mingling with people of different cultures. I guess it goes back to my days at Bloomfield Tech, where we had a very racially diverse school, so fitting in with other cultures has always come easy to me.

After visiting Ferry Street (and of course getting in one more good meal for the road), I had to visit the Downtown/Broad and Market area. This is the area where I have spent the vast majority of my career. I couldn't say good-bye to the job without coming here for one last swan song. I have more memories here than even I can remember. I must have walked around to every store downtown for a visit, and why not? I knew all of the owners; many of them I've known for years. Some stores have had several different owners over the years, and I believe I've known them all. Even the drug boys came up to me to say good-bye on this day. Many of them were just happy to see me go, and with good reason, because I've locked up enough of them. But on this day, I believe it was all about respect. I appreciated the respect I got from everyone this day, regardless of their walk of life. This cop job can be a thankless profession; it always helps to see somebody did appreciate your work. I like to think in some small way, I did make a difference out there.

5-May-2014

Partners for Life

AS I MENTIONED PREVIOUSLY, COMING UP AS an only child in the urban jungle of Newark's notorious Central Ward was a bitch. Things get hectic as hell in the Bricks if you got no backup. I had plenty of backup with my family, but my old man kept me away from them. So for a long time, it felt like I was alone. One dude who always had my back was my main man, Marcus "Fifty Grand" Peterson; we met in first grade, and we've been boys ever since. He had my back and took stands with me when nobody else would; he is my brother from another mother. He had my back in school, he had my back going home from school, and he had my back in the hood (well, that is, whenever I did come outside). We probably both hit it off because we were our parents' only children. So since we didn't have any brothers, we adopted each other.

Marcus loved basketball coming up, and he had some talent. When you could play basketball well during my era or you were a good athlete in general, it was a big plus in the hood. Most people saw sports as one of the few ways we could get out of the hood, so as an athlete, you had a certain status. So Marcus's status was significantly better than mine, which turned out to be a good thing for me; thanks to his status, he was able to talk some of my beefs away. Man, let me tell you, this kid got me out of a lot of shit.

Like the time these two pieces of shit from my building were fucking with me. One was this dude named Sheriff; he was a real low-life sack of shit. We had a couple of confrontations when we were kids growing up. I think he wanted to make a name for himself by fighting one of the bigger kids, so to make a long story short, we got into it on the playground, and being that he was a scrawny little motherfucker, I naturally put him on his ass. I guess he never got over it, so that's probably why we had trouble in the future.

The other asshole was an African nigga called Chilli Mu; this kid was a drug dealer/robber/burglar. He was a disease on the entire neighborhood; he was what you would call an accident waiting to happen to some unfortunate individual he would come across. So as I was coming home from high school on this nice spring day, I saw Sheriff and Chilli Mu walking down the street, and I noticed they were staring a hole through me as I walked by. When you see niggas staring too hard, the senses start going off because you know something is up. So at that point, I was really getting sick of niggas coming at me on some bullshit. So I stopped in my tracks, looked back at them, and yelled, "What's up? What's the problem?"

They just laughed at me and kept staring, so I just kept walking. I didn't think nothing of it until the next day; as I was going to school, they started following me. It caused me some concern because I knew of their reputations. Sheriff was known for carrying guns, and he had allegedly shot this dude in the foot while attempting a robbery in East Orange earlier that year. I tried to just ignore them, but every time I would see them, they would stare me down and then start following me. I mentioned this to my boy Marcus, who was knew both of these goons. Marcus was no punk, but he was not a thug either, but being that he was a good athlete, he knew a lot of people in the hood. So Marcus spoke to this dude they called Loop; he was a tall, muscular dude who had done a few bits in jail himself, but he was a good-hearted dude who looked out for the good kids from the neighborhood. He spoke to Sheriff and Chilli, and after that, I didn't have any more trouble from them. Marcus often joked with me when we got older and I became a cop; he used to say he had my back when we were younger, but now that we were, older I watched his back. But isn't that what real friends are for, watching each other's backs?

Once we got out of high school, Marcus and I lost contact. He went to Jersey State College and played basketball, and I was working and going to Essex County College at night, so our schedules were both full. We still manage to check on each other when time permits. He's my brother, so I'm never gonna totally lose contact with him; it's just we were older and had certain responsibilities now. Marcus and I are still very close; to this day, we hang out frequently, and our families are just like one family. I've seen in this life if you have a good friend who is in your corner no matter what, you are truly blessed. No one should live in the world alone.

When I was a cop, it was essential to find a good partner. That's half of this job. Usually, you will have more than one partner over your career; people get transferred, make rank, or take other jobs, so it's rare to keep the same partner your entire career. I've been fortunate enough to have a few good partners in my tenure, and most of them were women.

One partner who stands out for me is Wayne Jordan; he was a good dude, a real brother from the hood, just like me. He grew up in the South Ward of Newark, went to Shabazz High School and Essex County College, and was around the same age as me. This was my version of my boy Marcus on the Newark Police Department, the difference being that I was now a big strong officer of the law, so we had each other's back all day, every day. We worked together for three years. Going around the clock was certainly made a lot easier with a good partner. We usually patrolled the housing project areas in the East District. We soon gained a reputation in the projects for being hard but fair. We didn't play on the streets; we busted people for guns, drugs, domestic violence, robberies, burglaries. But Wayne and I were both from the hood, so we understood when to turn it up and when to be understanding because ultimately, your goal as a cop is to help your community. The fact that Wayne and I were both young when we came on the job helped us to get along, in particular when we were off duty. We worked hard and played even harder. Days off we were in the clubs and go-go bars, and when the four-to-twelve shift came around, we turned it up every day of the four-day tour. We were young and some real dogs.

One night at the Jetway Lounge on Sixteenth Avenue, we met these two girls at the bar. Wayne and I had just gotten off the four-to-twelve shift, and it was payday, so we went out after work for a little play and recreation. We met these two freaks, and after buying a couple of rounds of drinks, we were horny as hell, and the two freaks were even hornier than us, if that's possible. We ended up back at Wayne's apartment, and we went through three packs of condoms. We took turns on each girl; your partners are supposed to share (lmao). After working all night, then drinking and fucking the rest of the night, we were tired as hell, so we both booked off the next day. I know it looked suspicious, but real partners stick together through thick and thin.

Wayne was a hell of a partner, and Marcus is my brother till the end; however, the most loved and cherished partner I will ever have in my life is my beautiful wife, Jennifer (also known affectionately as Fudgy); she is my sun, moon, and stars. She has most definitely withstood the test of time. She has been by my side and in my life in one way or another for the last twenty years. We started off friends, became lovers, got engaged, and are now husband and wife. I can't thank Allah enough for putting her in my life. We have had our ups and downs, but at the end of the day, she's been with me in spite of my shit and in spite of my past when coming to the ladies, if you know what I mean. Another great quality she has is that when I give her the praise that she definitely deserves for dealing with my flaws and standing tall with me, she is just as quick to remind me how I have supported her over the years as well. That's ultimately what partners and soul mates do: We watch out for each other.

6-May-2014

Temptation

THE DEFINITION OF "TEMPTATION" IS THE STRONG urge or desire to do something, in particular something wrong or unwise. All of us have temptation in our lives in some shape or form. Temptation is everywhere, but in the urban hoods, temptation is almost like breathing; it is constant and continuous, and there is almost no letup. Temptations can beat you down and break your will. It takes a strong soul to avoid the many temptations that are in the hood. I know there will be individuals who read this and say people in the suburbs face their share of temptations as well, and I'm not trying to say that they don't. I'm just saying their temptations are not like those in the urban ghettos, where poverty is sadly a way of life. I mentioned before how close my parents kept me to them when I was growing up, but they couldn't keep me with them 24/7, so at some point, it's gonna come down to choices that individuals must make for themselves.

As a teenager, I had the temptation of stolen cars. I never personally stole a car myself, but several of my dudes were car thieves. My boy Kev (aka Crazy K) was good at stealing cars; this nigga was so crazy, he even drove some of the cars to school like it was his car. He lived in the Vailsburg area of Newark, which was halfway decent back then. He would steal cars from Maplewood, the Ivy Hill section of Newark, Union, anywhere he thought they had money and nice rides. He would offer to drive me home from school some days, and at first I turned him down, until this one warm spring day, he pulled up to the corner in a cherry Mercedes 300 series. I couldn't hold out no longer; he drove me all the way home. You should have seen the looks we got from the high school girls as we were driving by. At that time, they didn't have all of that LoJack technology to catch stolen cars, so if you knew how to drive and didn't do dumb shit in front of the police, you could get that off.

After I rode with him that time, I knew in my mind that I couldn't take too many more chances with him like that because all good things come to an end, and with my luck, I'd fuck around and get a charge, so I said no more (well, maybe just one more time). Me and Kev took one more joy ride for the road; we had already planned to skip school anyway, so Kev went out and got a car for us. At first, I had forgotten we were going to skip school. Kev came to school and reminded me a little before homeroom. So when we snuck out of school, I saw that Kev had already picked up the car. In the back of my mind, I knew I shouldn't be in that car with him. I knew I shouldn't be skipping school, I knew all the trouble I could get into, most important I knew what kind of problems I would have at home if I got into trouble. It's just that damn temptation is so hard to resist. Can't blame it on peer pressure; maybe it was the devil inside of me. No matter how much my mind told me it was wrong, my feet took control and walked me into that car.

So Kev and me set out on a journey; that day, we must have rode all over Essex County: East Orange, Orange, Newark, Irvington, Bloomfield. If the town was somewhat close, we rode through it. I have to say, although I knew what I was doing was wrong, that was one of the most exciting and adventurous days of my life. Living on the edge, not knowing if we were gonna get caught or go to jail was a big adrenaline rush; until that point in my life, I never felt more alive. After riding around most of the morning and early afternoon, we started to get hungry, so we stopped at the McDonald's on Dodd Street in East Orange. That's when I had my first run-in with the police.

While we were sitting down to eat, I noticed these two grown men kept looking at us; this was unlike my previous experiences with niggas staring at me. I didn't get the impression that they were checking us out for robbery or nothing sinister; they were giving us that look you would get from an adult or chaperone when they knew you were up to no good. As we were leaving McDonald's, the two men approached us. I immediately went on the defensive. I backed up with my fists balled up, and Kev yelled out to the dudes, "What you need? What's up?"

Before we could make matters worse, the two men introduced themselves as plainclothes cops; my heart started running like a race horse. I just knew I was going to jail. The officers put us in the back seat of the car and started questioning us; they asked us what school we went to, how old were we, where did we live: all of the basics. They scared us up good; they told us they worked for the robbery unit in Orange and we looked like some suspects wanted for a robbery.

They took us on a ride that seemed to last forever, but I noticed they didn't mention anything about the stolen ride. Finally, I heard them answer their car radio. When it was all said and done, they dropped us off in the Bloomfield Center and told us that they knew we were juveniles and we had skipped school; they also told us the only reason they weren't gonna take this any further is because they had an important call.

Before they let us go, they told us they would call the school so we better take our asses back. Well, we couldn't go back because by the time they finished with us, it was after school, so we just went on about our business. I told Kev we were lucky they never saw us get out of the car; they just looked at us and saw we were high school kids. I beat the wheel that day, and after that, I never wanted to get in or near a stolen car.

My boy Kev continued with the stolen cars for a while; I think he even went back to get that car that day (lol). Once he graduated school, he stopped, realizing he was a grown man now and it was time to grow up. Wow, how my life could have changed for the worse if I had been caught in a stolen ride. I must again give all praise to God for guiding me from danger and giving me the strength to resist further temptation. Temptation even found me after becoming a cop. I spoke previously about how after becoming a cop, you suddenly have a lot of these friends and acquaintances you never had before.

Well, after becoming a cop, I had drug boys from the hood who wouldn't even look my way before because they considered me to be a geek, a straight arrow, not the type of nigga they could fuck with growing up, but now they wanted to be cool, and some of them now wanted to hang out. They used come at me and say, "Yo, Hakim, let's swing out to Marlo's or Club American; it's on me. I got you."

I'd just politely turn them down and keep it moving. I already knew the only thing hanging out with them would get me is prosecuted or in the unemployment line for fraternizing with a known criminal element. Sorry, not going to happen.

I even had some cats who were decent with me growing up, but they always did their little one-twos on the side for extra cash; they asked me if I wanted to make some extra money on the low by putting money toward their drug endeavors. My answer to them was, "Hell no, are you crazy? No way I'm gonna jeopardize what I have for chump change; if you ain't at least talking about something that's gonna get a nigga 5.5 million, it's no sense in us even talking about this shit." Keeping it real: Even large money like that is not worth having to always look over your shoulder. I'm not gonna take the risk of my mother having to visit me in jail. As a patrolman on the street, temptation still had a way of reaching out and trying to get ahold of me.

One day while working as a one-man unit, I was on Jefferson Street giving out double parking tickets; this Brazilian lady came up to me after I had just ticketed her car. She asked me if I could take the ticket back, but I explained that was not possible. She then said that if I came back to her house later, then maybe she could talk me into taking the ticket back. I told her, "I'm gonna pretend that we never had this conversation because if I didn't, I would have to lock you up."

So she quickly saw the error of her ways. Temptation will challenge us all at some point, so keep your guard up and be ready.

7-May-2014

A Mother's Love

ALTHOUGH WE MAY NOT HAVE SEEN EYE to eye on a number of matters over the years, in particular when it came to my father, my mother has always been my backbone and my heart. I know I may have resented the way she smothered me as a child, and I often had to advise to take it easy with the smothering as an adult, but at the end of the day, she was always there for me. She was often hard on me coming up, but in my neighborhood, you had to be hard on your kids because if you didn't, the streets would be even harder on them. I was her only child, and she was determined to make sure that I had a proper upbringing. She often went against my father's wishes when she had to, in order to make me happy. Over the years, she has helped me through some shaky moments, even after I became a police officer. When I came on the job, I was young, dumb, and full of cum, and I often blew money on partying and the ladies. For a minute, I was out of control.

During this time, I fell into my share of financial difficulties, but through it all, I could count on Mom. She was the glue that kept our family together; my father would have been nothing without her, and I can say without shame I wouldn't be shit without her either. I always give praise first and foremost to Allah, my lord and master; he is most merciful for allowing my mother to be here with me as long as he has, and I continue to ask every day that he keep her here a bit longer.

I truly saw what an angel my mother was when my father was sick; she stood by him until the day he died. At the time, I didn't think he deserved it, but I know now it's not my call to say who deserves what in this life and certainly not who deserves what in the next life. That call is for the creator only. So as good as he has been to me, I'm not going to overstep my bounds. I just pray that Allah gives me the time and the means to give my mother a good life for the rest of her days. A mother's love is unconditional and lasts for life. No one will ever love you like your mother. I see how some of these young kids disrespect their mothers, and I'm like, "Wow, you don't realize you only get one mother; you should cherish her. Yes, she's going to get on your nerves; that's her job. She keeps you on your toes by doing that. It's all done out of love, you can certainly bet on that. I can say without a shadow of a doubt I can count on Mom when I can't count on anyone else. As an adult, I now feel very protective toward my mother; that's the main reason why I stayed close to my parents all of these years. It certainly wasn't to help my father. You know that's still something I have to work on. Allah will judge my father, not me. Hatred only poisons one's heart and soul; I pray to God that he will give me the strength to rise higher. If anyone deserves a special place on heaven, in my opinion, it's my mom; her faith in God is unshakable, and her heart is as big as the Pacific Ocean.

When I was younger, we stayed on the eighth floor in Brick Towers, and my mother was like the mother of the eighth floor. She would often look out for the kids who didn't have a strong parental influence in their lives. Many of the kids in my age range had a great deal of respect for my mother, and they would often come to her for advice when they didn't have anyone else to talk to. As a kid, you sometimes don't realize how blessed you are to have someone special in your life; just being honest, even as grown adults, we often don't appreciate the good that God gives us but always remember, as long as we're blessed to see another day with a loved one, that is another day we're given an opportunity to show them how much we love them. So be blessed and take advantage of that opportunity.

Some may say that my mother was too protective of me when I was growing up, and maybe she was; you know how it is: You have to let your birds leave the nest at some point. You have to allow children to experience certain things in life so they can grow as people and learn how to exist for themselves in this world. No one is perfect, and no matter how good your intentions may be, everyone makes mistakes. I know for a fact whatever mistakes my mother made, her attentions were only the best for me. With all the emotional pain and drama that once consumed my life, it was a wonder that I made to adulthood, let alone to where I am now. No, not really. I know what God me by my Lord and a mother's love.

8-May-2014

A New Chapter

IT's THE MORNING OF OCTOBER 18; THE year is 2016. I'm headed out to open new doors in my life, to try and accomplish a goal I've had since childhood: to become a journalist. I'm now ready to start a new career at the ripe young age of forty-seven. I feel great, I feel relaxed, unlike when I started out as a cop. I don't feel any fear or apprehension; why should I? I now have a stable pension coming in every month, I'm married with a family, I'm taking care of Mama; thank God her health is good, so I'm at a much more stable place in life than I was over twenty-five years ago, plus with age, you start to lose that sense of fear over time. Think about it: After doing twenty-five years in Newark as a cop, what else could ever put fear in me? For the first year after retirement, I did the usual cop thing: I worked part time three days a week, doing armed security here and there for a little play money. I really just wanted to relax a little while; after spending two decades on the streets of Newark, I was burned out, so I needed some me time to revitalize my mind and soul.

And I was able to do that with my pension and part-time work; also, I'm blessed to have a wife who is a nurse, making good money, so I'm blessed in that regard. After a while, however, I said to myself, *Hakim, it's time to start making some moves, and I mean some real power moves.* I had my degree, so I said, "It's time to make it work for me." So one brisk fall morning, I headed over to Manhattan to interview for a position at CNN.

I was dressed to the max, and I just recently had my resume redone. I was excited as hell. Everything about this morning felt so right; you ever have a feeling that you just know it's gonna be a good morning, and everything is gonna go your way? Well, if you have, then you know how I felt. I toasted myself a bran muffin and had some green tea for breakfast, and then I was off to Penn Station, heading toward New York. The train was filled with passengers but also peaceful; I read the *Newark Star Ledger* as we traveled over the tracks through Jersey City and Hoboken, and finally we stop at Penn Station in Manhattan.

I've always loved traveling to New York with all of the sights and the people; I've always found it so exciting. New York is a city where anybody and everybody can just blend in and be themselves, unlike certain parts of New Jersey, where it seems like everybody is always trying to fit in to this clique or that clique instead of just being themselves. When I approached the tall, luxurious building on 10 Columbus Circle, my eyes lit up like a Christmas tree. I thought to myself, *If I get up in here, not only am I gonna be in a whole different tax bracket, but this job will take my life to another level. I'm gonna travel and see the world; think about the connections I'm gonna make.*

As I rode up the elevator for my interview on the 50th floor, mind feeing with the wonderful opportunities the job would present to me, I couldn't help but think back to all of my beloved family members I had lost over the years. I thought, *Wow, if they could only see me now.* But first I had to get the job.

I walked off the elevator and sat down in the waiting room until it was time to go in for the interview. I sat there watching *Good Morning* America on one of the flat screens while sipping some French vanilla coffee. The waiting area was very impressive, just like the whole building. I never saw so many different pastries and bagels; they had trays and pans of everything you could want for breakfast. Every style of eggs you could want, a variety of breakfast meats, toast, waffles, pancakes; you name it, it was there. I didn't indulge, though. I was only concentrating on this interview. All of this food looked great, but if I ate this good in the morning, I might get a case of the itis, so I didn't wanna take that chance. I wanted to be on point like a motherfucker when I went in there to speak to the man.

It was ten o'clock, time for my interview. I walked down the hall toward the office, confident in my Brooks Brothers dark blue suit, my black Stacy Adams shoes, and my navy blue silk tie. I was sharp and alert, and after twenty-five years of policing in Newark, I was ready for anything. The interview was with Arthur Hilgeman, the assistant director of personnel for this branch at CNN. Our interview lasted for about forty-five minutes. I felt a good vibe from my responses to his different questions during that interview. I used some of my police experience from being cross-examined during trials and testifying in front of a judge. I was calm and collected; I gave full, direct answers but also made it a point to show him the witty, engaging side of my personality. After the interview, I left his office with a good feeling about what had taken place during our talk. I had to stop back at the waiting room before I left the building; now that the interview was over, it was time to get into all of that delicious food (lol).

Two weeks went by before I heard from CNN; they sent me an email to come in for a second interview, so a few days before Thanksgiving, I went back to Manhattan. After going back to the 50th floor to speak to Mr. Hilgeman, he told me the awesome news: I was now a journalist for CNN. I felt so good leaving that building; the ride home on the train was one of the best rides of my life. My mind was racing all over the place, thinking about this great job, this great salary, and all the great benefits. When I made it home, I broke the incredible news to my wife and my mom; they were ecstatic. I could hardly sleep that night; my adrenaline was pumping. This was an awesome start to the rest of my life.

9-May-2014

JANUARY 5, 2017, WAS MY FIRST DAY at CNN, the first day of a new career, a new life, the first day at the next level. After I walked into the building, I got into the elevator and headed up to my office on the 75th floor. I started reflect back to those days in the courtyard of Brick Towers; it was like during that whole elevator ride from the lobby to the 75th floor, my whole childhood went through my mind: Brick Towers, the strip mall on West Kinney and MLK Blvd., 32 Flavors on Court and MLK (man, they had a walnut milk shake that was off the chain), the record store, and Mr. West's Bakery. I also thought about my first day at St. Mary's Elementary; all of this passed through my mind in that quick journey. I'm like wow I'm in a building with a hundred floors; as a youngster, I thought Hill Manor at 611 MLK Blvd. was a tall building with twenty-five floors, but this bad boy is a skyscraper for real.

My first day in this corporation was completely the opposite of my first day with the Newark Police Department. There were no intimidating drill sergeants trying to draw fear from you or break your will; oh no, instead, there were beautiful receptionists and administrative assistants who looked like they could have been contestants on *America's Next Top Model;* they greeted me and welcomed me to the company. The main focus of the first few days was giving me an orientation of the company and explaining what my job consisted of.

I could tell this type of work was meant for me. As much as I enjoyed policing, I often found myself looking at the clock to see how many hours I had left before my day was over, something that most people do regardless of what type of work they do. Today, however, for the first time in my life, I felt the total opposite. I actually looked at the clock hoping I had more time left at work. I was totally in my comfort zone with this gig. NPD was wonderful, but as they used to say on the block, "This was my shit." I didn't have to follow a chain of command to meet the supervisors; in fact, the president and the vice president of this branch of the company called me into their offices to meet them. My cubical was not huge, but it felt way more comfortable than a radio car. My phones and computers were state-of-the-art; the carpeting was luxurious; and the view from the windows was breathtaking. Man, I felt like George Jefferson because I really had moved on up. I was like a kid in a candy store; admittedly, I wasn't used to this. My first fourteen years as a cop, all we had were old, outdated typewriters.

They really knew how to welcome a brother to the company. I said to myself, So this is how the other half lives. I was damn sure basking in the moment. I wasn't going to fool myself; I knew every day was not gonna be like this one. I could only imagine how hectic the job could get, but at least I was doing my lifetime passion, so I was eager to see if what I heard is true: if your job consists of doing something you really love, it's like you're not really working. I was more pumped up for this than when I was a rookie cop, and why not? Life had experienced me for anything. I couldn't wait to combine my education along with my police experience for my new position. After the first day ended, as I took the train home, I had to give all praise and glory to God; he blessed me to be in a position to do what I love, and I was more determined than ever not to let him or myself down. When you come from nothing and you finally get a break in this life, you had better make it count.

10-May-2014

MAKING THE TRANSITION FROM LAW ENFORCEMENT to reporting wasn't as difficult as I thought it would be; even though I was never a detective or had any certified investigative training, I adapted quite well to my new job. Then again, when you really look into it, there are some similarities between reporting and policing. You do a lot of writing in both fields, you interview people as a reporter, and over the years I can't count how many victims and suspects I've interviewed as a cop, so both fields have a number of things in common. One of the biggest differences being now as a reporter, I can't lock a person up for lying to me (lol). Believe me, some of the people I interview now, I can look right into their eyes and see that they're lying, but my job is to report the news and just take their statements, which works for me. It's somebody else's job to make a case against them if they're doing something wrong.

One of my biggest concerns after retiring from the police department was the fear of being burned out. You know, twenty-five years of the whole paramilitary thing, along with working those busy streets of Newark, had me feeling a little drained toward the end. That's how I knew this reporting thing was for me because right from the beginning of this job I felt refreshed again. It was almost like this work revitalized me. Reinventing yourself is good for you in every way. I know one thing: I have to stay away from all the temptation that's around me, and by that I mean the women; that's always been my downfall in the past. I'm married and love my wife with every fiber of my being, but this is going to be a little tough. These young women around the business district make the ladies I used to see at

Broad and Market look like last week's leftover trash, and that's not even mentioning the women in this hundred-floor building; like I said before, these ladies could be on TV.

Thankfully, I have my faith and my beautiful family to help keep me grounded. Plus, I'm here to concentrate on work; all of this eye candy is just one of the benefits of this job. It can't hurt to look, can it? I'm working on this story about, of all things, police corruption in Brookline, a suburb on the outskirts of Boston, a quite insignificant area at first glance but a town that supposedly has been plagued by corrupt policing for years. I was told by my supervisor that when the assignment first came in, the executives upstairs immediately thought of giving the job to me, considering my background in law enforcement. At first, I was a little apprehensive (you know, the whole cop loyalty thing), but then it occurred to me that I handled plenty of jobs that I was a little uncomfortable with but did them because it was my job, after all, not personal.

So the company paid for me to go to Brookline for one week to gather information for the story. They also sent an assistant down there with me. Her name was Elaina Cortez, and right from the door, I knew I was in trouble. Elaina was five feet nine inches in height and about 150 pounds over the most curvy, well-toned frame; she was the most sensuous Puerto Rican you'd every wanna lay eyes on. I thought, *Good God almighty, why are they doing this to me?* She was so fine, if you just walked in a room with her, women would just automatically get jealous of her and men would look at you like you were the man.

We stayed at this small motel off of Route 9 in Brookline (of course, we had separate rooms). The first few days, we went around asking questions and taking statements from the people who initially started the complaints against the police. We spoke to citizens and business owners, but most importantly (for me at least), I wanted to speak to the police and get their side of this story as well. I knew it may be difficult to get direct statements from officers because some police departments let officers speak to the media and some don't. So I started with the people in charge, like the mayor and the chief of police. I tried to make them feel at ease by mentioning to them that

I used to be a police officer. I noticed, however, they were still some-what distant with me, as was some of the general public.

What can you do? I guess after the police, reporters are next when it comes to people feeling uneasy around them. After a few day of investigating, I received an unexpected and most unwanted gift, which someone left in front of my motel room door. At first, my policing training told me to call it in as a suspicious package because it seemed a little odd to me. But then I thought, *Who knows; maybe it's a gift from Elaina.* After all, we had a good vibe working together this week. Getting a gift from her would be good for my ego, but it would open too many doors that would lead to trouble for me. My curiosity started killing me after a while, so I just opened the package and found a dead rat in with a letter that said, "Mind your business, nigger, and everything will be all right."

You talk about a brother being mad as hell. I called the police (even though I hate to admit it, but they were the top on my suspect list who else would have the resources to find out so quickly where I was staying). They came out and took a report for me; one of the officers asked me sarcastically if I was afraid; that's when that Central Ward shit started coming out of me. I told them I'm just trying to cover my ass with this report, and I had to remind them that I'm a retired officer and as such I'm authorized to carry a weapon myself, so if anyone came at me in a way where I had to defend myself, they're gonna get something they don't want. After the cops left, I told Elaina, and she flipped out; the whole thing had us shook up pretty good. I tried to relax her and said that we already had most of what we needed for the story, which we did, because as I said before, we worked well together and got a lot done in a little time.

We ended up at another hotel a bit farther down the highway. After a long day, I was tired so I was about to turn in early when I hear somebody knocking frantically on my door. I went to the door with my .40 caliber in my right hand, just in case. I opened the door slowly and saw that it was Elaina; she was still shaken up, so I tried to calm her down. We spent next hour talking and sipping some wine. As we talked and sipped, I couldn't help but notice how good Elaina was looking; she had on a white blouse with some jeans that fitted those gorgeous hips like a glove, not to mention some clear stilettos that only enhanced everything, if you know what I mean.

After we talked, Elaina appeared to have calmed down, so eventually we started talking about life in general. I told her about my family and certain details about my life in general, and she did the same; the only difference was, she wasn't married. The conversation got to be deep and heavy, and when I looked at the clock, it was now one in the morning. I didn't wanna seem rude, but I had to tell baby girl that it was getting late; just as she was about to leave my room, she turned around and gave me a hug; now, why did she do that? The hug led to a kiss on the cheek, which led to another hug, which ended up with her spending the rest of the night in my room, and we weren't talking, if you know what I mean.

11-May-2014

THE NEXT MORNING, I WOKE UP WITH a smoking hot Latina cuddled up next to me, with her head on my chest. I look at her and thought, *Oh my God, she is just as fine when she's sleeping as she is when she's awake.* Then I looked at that pretty olive skin, the long jet-black hair, that scrumptious shapely body with a pair of legs to die for. Most men would envy the hell out of me for waking up in a position like that. Back in my heyday, that would have been an ideal ending to a good evening, but at this point in my life, I felt like a total piece of shit. I tried to play it off when baby girl woke up, but after a while, she could tell I was feeling a certain way about what happened last night. After we got dressed and packed our things, we went out for breakfast before we went to the train station.

Over breakfast, it was a little uncomfortable at first, then after the initial awkwardness eased, we discussed our situation. The more we talked, the better I felt. Elaina was very cordial and diplomatic about the whole thing. She told me that she understood my situation with my wife and child and said that she would never want to have an adverse effect on my family. She told me that we both just got caught up in the moment; she also made it clear that while she wasn't trying to take me from my wife, that we were both mature adults. She was interested in continuing an adult friendship with me, as long as we kept it between us, on the downlow.

Here I was, approaching fifty years of age, and I had a thirty-one-year-old quarter piece sitting in front of me, offering an opportunity any man of any age would jump at, and I was sitting there looking like a chicken with its head cut off. As comforting as her words were to me, I still felt like a heel. I had a beautiful wife and an adoring child at home. I know I must be getting old now; back in the day, I would have loved a situation like this: a chance to have my cake and eat it, but I was more domesticated. The whole train ride home, I felt so bad. I kept thinking about how I could end up losing my family and everything I had worked so hard to finally get. It took me forever to get a wife and child, and I would lose my mind if I lost it for one night of passion.

Elaina could see it on my face so she tried her best to reassure me that it was gonna be okay. She said, "Honey, stop worrying. I'm not gonna say nothing; you're driving yourself crazy for no reason."

It wasn't even the possibility of getting caught that worried me; it was me thinking about what I did to my wife. As I got off the train, I started thinking of ways to justify my adultery. I thought to myself how it wasn't all my fault; a man has needs. Jennifer and I had been together for years, and she is beauty, but let's say, for example, I love steak, but as much as I like it, I don't wanna eat steak every day.

Also, sometimes in relationships, a gorgeous black woman can get complacent, and she just relies on her natural beauty to arouse her man. Sisters have to realize that variety is the spice of life, and sometimes these women of others races are a bit more creative when it comes to sex and how to seduce a man. Women may not like to admit it, but sex is a vital part of a relationship. They say the way to a man's heart is through his stomach. I say if you want to keep your man in the house, you need to learn how to work those lips and jaw muscles and how to work that pussy.

When it was all said and done, no matter how many excuses I came up with in my mind, I still felt lower than dirt because I knew I had done wrong: no ifs, ands, or buts. The whole train ride home, I struggled with my conscience and debated whether I should come clean to Jennifer or not.

I talked it over with my best friend, Marcus Peterson; yes, we are still boys after over forty years. I finally came to the conclusion that the only right thing and best thing to do was to keep my mouth shut. Sometimes what you don't know can't hurt you, just like as a cop when I would advise people of their rights; the right to remain silent is often very beneficial for me, so in this case, it was in my family's best interests that I exercised that right.

12-May-2014

SEVERAL WEEKS WENT AFTER I HAD MY little one-nighter with Elaina; since then, everything was pretty much back to normal. When I got home, I greeted my wife with a big kiss and hug, and then I gave another big hug to my wonderful son, Amir, who is now three years old and running all over the place, and can this kid talk up a storm; he amazes me every day. I'm so in awe over how smart he is; I jokingly tell Jennifer that he must have gotten it from her because I don't think I was anywhere near as sharp or receptive as he is. I kept my game face on; like I said, what happens in Brookline, stays in Brookline. I have a happy and beautiful family life. I had just one lapse in judgment, one moment of weakness; a man shouldn't be hung for one slip-up. The way I see it, no harm, no foul. After I got back from Brookline, I took my family out for dinner over to City Island in the Bronx. I missed being with my loved ones that week, so I wanted to make up for that lost time. We had a great time at dinner, and afterward, we came home and watched movies for the rest of the evening. And after putting our son to bed, Jennifer and I made love. It was the weekend, so we were off from work the next day. I took advantage of this weekend and spent as much time as I could with my wife and kid; maybe I looked at this like it was my penance for what I had done.

After the weekend, I returned to work on Monday, feeling much more relaxed and comfortable in my skin than I was a few days ago; it was back to business as usual. I was glad to have a heavy case load laid out for me because I always like to stay busy; it makes time go faster, plus it just made me feel more productive to be busy rather than sitting around with nothing to do. It also kept my mind off certain things.

When I went out for lunch, I saw Elaina on the elevator. She smiled at me with that sparkling smile of hers; we spoke briefly after exiting the elevator and then went on our separate ways, which was a good thing for me because the last thing I needed was to have lunch with her at a time when I was trying keep away from all of my lower desires.

Several weeks went by, and everything seemed perfectly normal, both at home and work, so I just continued to do what I do: work, gym, mosque, home, and family. I saw Elaina many times, and we were friendly as always. She often reminded me that her offer was still open, for me to be her silent lover on the lowdown if I wanted to. She was a real down-to-earth girl who kept it real. She told me it wasn't about falling in love; she liked the dick. You can only imagine what that did for a brother's ego; that was until I asked her a question I now regret asking. I just had to ask her if she really found me that attractive.

Elaina is a straight shooter, so she told me honestly that I was okay as far as looks go. She told me what attracted her to me was my personality and (of course) my eyes, but the main reason she wanted to continue our sexual relationship wasn't because of my looks, it was that dick. So with that being said, I was interested in her proposal. I'm not going to lie, but I knew at this point my conscience wouldn't let me give in; it took every bit of discipline I had in me to resist. She was looking so good that day; what am I talking about? This bitch looks hot as hell every day. So many perverted thoughts went through my mind when I was talking to her; the thought of being able to have my sexy chocolate wife, who is eye candy herself, and then on the side for dessert, I can have this lovely, delicious, butter-pecan Latina. A man would have to be a fool not to take an offer like this. I'm a grown man now; God forgives, but if you keep doing the same thing over and over again, eventually your luck is going to run out. A few more weeks went by. Life was going pretty smooth, which is when I start to worry because it seems like whenever things are going too smooth, some crazy shit is usually around the corner, so get ready.

I noticed one other thing: during this period, I didn't see Elaina. I figured she was probably on an assignment somewhere or just busy doing whatever. I must have thought her up, as they say, because the very next day, I saw her at a local diner where I often go to lunch. She told me she knew that the diner was one of my favorite spots and that she was hoping to see me. Several thoughts went through my mind when said this to me; first, I'm thinking maybe she wants to make a brother another proposal. Another thought that went through my mind was this chick must have really been turned out by my manhood down there, so maybe she is not gonna take no for an answer. So finally I just said to myself, *Relax. Stop putting crazy thoughts in the universe; just sit back, relax, and let her say what she got to say.*

13-May-2014

THE CONVERSATION STARTED OFF INNOCENTLY ENOUGH: HOW is the family, how's work, the usual. Then just as she was about to get the main topic, the waitress came for our order. I ordered a garden salad and salmon cakes; Elaina ordered a grilled chicken Caesar salad. After ordering, and with all the other distractions out of the way, she was ready to get to the point. She asked if I had noticed not seeing her in the past few weeks. I played it off and said I had thought of her, but I had been so busy, I didn't know sometimes if I was going or coming. She then told me why I hadn't seen her: She said she had been experiencing some stomach problems and other women problems, as she put it.

When she said this, I immediately became concerned, so I interrupted her and asked about her health. She said she was fine, the symptoms weren't serious, but they did make her go to the doctor to see if everything was okay. From there, she told me what the doctor said: that she was pregnant. My face dropped to the floor; the doctor said she was seven weeks along, and my mind thought back to when we had our little one-nighter. So I had to ask the million-dollar question: "Is the baby mine?"

I told her no disrespect intended, but until we hooked up for that week in Brookline, I had never met her or knew anything about her, like if she had a boyfriend, a lover, or anyone before me or after me. She told me no offense taken, she understood news like this was not something you just digest easily. She understood how a man in my situation would want to know beyond a shadow of a doubt if that was his child. I thanked her for being so understanding and everything. I told I remembered using protection, so I was a little confused; she reminded me that there was a point during that wild night of passion where the condom did break, and as soon as she mentioned that, it came back to me. She was right; it did break, but I was in her pussy so deep and intense, I could not stop. I thought I pulled it out in time, but who knows?

Elaina told me she was willing to take a blood test; she added that she broke up with her boyfriend two months before we did anything, and she hadn't been with anyone until me or after me; in fact, she half-jokingly said that may have contributed to her being so intense in bed with me that night because she was horny. Okay, now that the initial shock and all of that was out of the way, I asked another important question: What could we do (or better, what would she like to be done) to possibly rectify this problem we had?

I told her that I was not trying to sound cold or heartless in any way toward her being pregnant, but we had to take into account both of our circumstances; for starters, until two months ago, we didn't know each other. Secondly, she had her career to think about, along with her side work in the modeling industry. She was planning to go back to school for her master's in communications. Her future goal was to be an anchor on one of the news channels.

We talked so much that neither us had a chance to eat, and lunch time was almost over, so we agreed to meet up after work and talk about this over dinner. All during the rest of the work day, no matter how busy I tried to keep myself, I couldn't shake what she had told me at lunch. I wondered how I could break this to my wife; I thought this was the end of my marriage. What kind of luck do I get? One little mistake could cost me everything it had taken me so long to get. I can't emphasize enough how all it takes is one fuck to send your life on a downward spiral. One other thing that stayed on my mind was, even if she got an abortion, how would that sit with my Lord and my faith? To be honest, this whole damn situation doesn't look good in my faith, period, from the adultery to the current problem.

Once the work day was over, it was like a big relief for me because now I could address the problem at hand. I lied to Jennifer and told her I had work late on an assignment. When I got to the diner, Elaina was already there and had a table for us; we ordered our meals and then proceeded to talk. This time, however, we ate while we talked; I guess both of us were hungry after missing lunch. We must have talked for about two hours easily; I again explained my side of things, and she was very understanding. (I couldn't help but think, Man, if I had met her before Jennifer, I would probably have married her; she is so understanding and easy to talk to.)

She told me how she felt and assured me that by no means did she wish to break up my family or cause me any trouble, but she also told me that while still a young woman, her biological clock was ticking, and even under these circumstances, she may not want to abort her baby. She needed a little time to think about it. It wasn't the answer I wanted, but I could see where she was coming from.

14-May-2014

As I waited for her answer, I must admit this problem was a constant thought in my head; during the course of the next few days, how could I not think about her decision? It could affect the rest of my life. Yes, it could, but life still goes on; things happen, but life is about making adjustments, no matter what happens. Just like when tragedy strikes in our life and we lose those who are near and dear to our heart, but tomorrow is still another day, and it will start and finish with or without you. So I did what I've always done when faced with adversity: keep on keeping on. I continued going to work and working hard; I went home to my family and did the family thing as always.

I needed someone to speak to on the matter, so I confided in my sister in faith, Sister Khadijah, who I have known since our days in the nation of Islam before we eventually converted to the more traditional Sunnah of Islam. Of course she gave me an ear full for my bad behavior (I'm glad she didn't know about my other sexual forays when I was younger). After reaming me a new one, she then began to comfort me by telling me that Allah loves to forgive and that he is the best to forgive me in a time like this. She also told me what I already knew, that if Elaina does decide to have the baby that I had to tell Jennifer everything. She went as far as to tell me that I should tell Jennifer everything even if Elaina decides not to have the baby.

I told her, "Let's not get carried away now." As a man, if she decides to have the baby, I'm going to step up and do what I should do. I would never be a deadbeat dad; I'm not made like that. I would help her take care of our child, and I would be in my child's life. I'm well aware that would mean telling my wife everything, which

I'm willing to do. I know what I did was wrong, so if the dice rolls that way, I have no other choice but to man up and deal with the consequences of my actions. One valuable bit of information Sister Khadijah did give me was in reference to abortions and Islam. She advised me that if it is done within the first month and a half of the pregnancy, the fetus does not have life yet, so there is no sin.

Either way, I was now mentally prepared for whatever decision Elaina made. Like I said, life is about making adjustments; if this doesn't work, then be ready to try something else. After a few more days went by, I received a call from Elaina, and we agreed to meet at the Livingston Mall on Saturday morning. As a married man, my weekends are usually tied up with the family, especially during the daytime, so I had to come up with yet another lie to meet up with her. This time, I told Jennifer I had a meeting to attend for work and would be tied up for a couple of hours. So I took a slow ride over to the mall; during the drive, I must have gone through every possible scenario in my head as to what the outcome of this meeting would be. I just got to a point where I said to myself, *It is what it is; besides, just take it easy and let everything play itself out.*

So I met her at the Barnes and Noble bookstore. We sat down and talked. This time, we didn't go through any formalities; we got straight to the point. Elaina told me that she decided to get an abortion. She thanked me for being patient with her and said that over the last few days, she thought about everything carefully. She thought of her career and her future plans and how having a baby right now was not a good move for her. She also said she took into account my family situation. She also shared the same beliefs I always had, because she would like to be married before she had a child. After speaking to her and taking another slow ride, this time going home, I felt light as a feather. It felt like the weight of the world was just lifted off of my shoulders. Wow, what a relief. I went home with a new pep in my step. I chilled out with the family that weekend and took it easy. Allah is so good; he may not always do what I ask when I ask, but he is always on time. And the rest of that weekend, I had to offer up extra prayers for thanks and for forgiveness. PS— I slept like a baby that weekend.

15-May-2014

I CHERISHED THE TIME I SPENT WITH MY son Amir this past weekend. Not that I don't cherish every moment that I'm with him. It's just this past weekend was so surreal. It made me appreciate my family even more than I already do. I might not have been caught, but I'm very aware of how my life could have changed if Elaina had made another decision in this matter. Amir will always be my son; I'm able to see him all day, every day if I want, but I wouldn't know how to act if I had to get visitation rights through a judge to see him (not to mention having to pay child support). And my wife, who I do love so dearly, the last thing I wanted to do was break her heart.

A close call like this can really bring a dude back to earth. That Monday when I went back to work, it was business as usual. I was determined to put that incident behind me and keep my eyes on the prize. I received my next assignment, which was on drug wars in Chicago, one of America's largest cities. I had never been to Chicago, I just knew of it what I saw and heard on TV. For this assignment, they gave me two assistants to help me gather information. One of them was an intern, a white kid studying journalism at NYU. Frank was a bright, articulate young man, well groomed, very polite, and handsome; the type of young man you could easily see being the face of some news station in the future. He was a semester short from getting his degree and was working at CNN to get some on-the-job experience. The second assistant was an older white woman named Donna, who had worked for the company for years. I was happy they put me with this team because after the last time, I did not want any tempting eye candy around me. With that being said, even if they had sent me another beauty to work with, after all the stress that I just went through, a chick would have to practically strap me down and drug me in order to get me to lay up with her.

When we arrived in Chicago, I could tell things were destined to run smoother than they did in Brookline. For starters, this time the police and law enforcement agencies were a bit more receptive to us (why wouldn't they be? After all, I wasn't here looking to investigate them; lol). The police were helpful in helping me gather crime statistics and other data that I needed for my report, and I really appreciated the security detail that they gave me when I told them that I needed to go into the heart of the hood in Chi-town. I like to get real-life accounts of the people who live on these streets, who have been personally affected by the culture of the drugs and violence.

First, I spoke to a grandmother, Mrs. Carla Chambers, who lost a daughter during the crack era. She told me her daughter was accidentally shot during a drug war that was going on at that time in the Cabrini Green Projects. She said she and her now-deceased husband raised eleven kids (seven boys and four girls) on the north side of Chicago. She told me how this area had been ravaged for the better part of three decades by drug gangs. I felt so bad for her because within the last year, she lost one of her grandsons due to a drive-by shooting; if that wasn't bad enough, another one of her grandsons is facing a murder charge in the retaliation shooting death of a young man he suspected was responsible for his cousin's death. Wow, talk about a twisted swing of fate.

I then went with my team to South Homan Avenue and West Roosevelt Road, one of the most notorious blocks in the entire country, not just Chicago. I spoke to the Brooks family. They are a young family of three. The husband, Kyle, is twenty-seven; his wife, Sharon, is twenty-four. They have been married for three years and have a two-year-old girl named Jessica, who is an absolute doll. They're both striving to get ahead. Kyle works as a mechanic at a local garage, and Sharon works as a security officer at a recycling plant on the east side of town. Both are hard-working people with goals and ambitions, but like a lot of young people in the hood, they're not making enough money to get over the hump, and with the skyrocketing cost of living, they can't get out of the hood.

I can definitely relate to their plight because, it was similar to mine when I was their age. All of us had finished high school and had some college, but we could not get up the money to finish college, so without that four-year degree, you were stuck in nowhere land, without enough education to get a higher paying job. They told me how they both would like to get into law enforcement. Sharon wants to be a corrections officer, and Kyle, God bless him, wants to be a city cop. In the meantime, however, they are living in a neighborhood where drugs and guns run wild. They said how often at night, their daughters lay in bed, trembling out of fear from hearing all the gunshots. Hearing these stories made me think of my hometown of Newark and how I felt sometimes as a child in my old neighborhood. Let's be honest: The hood is the hood, the game is the same; no matter where your hood is, the only thing that changes is the intensity of the game.

My trip to Chicago went very well. I gathered a lot of information with help of my assistants, and I had a feeling this was going to be one of my better reports. Who knows, this one could help put me up there with the big boys in this industry. It might win me one of those prestigious journalism awards. While I felt very satisfied with the business end of this trip, during the flight home, I couldn't help but think of those unfortunate individuals I met in Chicago: the grandmother who raised eleven kids and who helps bring up her twenty-five grandkids. I could feel some of the pain she has dealt with living in Chicago's urban hood. But in spite of her struggles, she keeps her family together, with a strong resolve and an even stronger faith in God. When you think about it, she is a real American hero.

Kyle and Jessica are a great example of young African Americans who continue to strive for success, no matter what obstacles come in front of them. They keep a positive outlook on life and are very devoted to their child and giving her a good upbringing, regardless of the conditions around them. True soldiers all of them.

16-May-2014

THE NEXT DAY AT WORK, AFTER RETURNING from Chicago, as I was finishing my story, I had an inspiration for another story that I felt needed to be put out there. I remembered when I was growing up in the Central Ward, no matter how rough certain blocks or neighborhoods were, you always had a lady in the hood who would take in foster kids from broken homes in an effort to give them some sense of family. The first person I thought of was my beloved grandmother, Mrs. Elawuese Tilery. While she never officially had any foster kids, she certainly went out of her way to help many of the young people in the neighborhood whose families had turned their backs on them. My granny was only in my life for three years, but the stories of her kindness were legendary, many years after she passed. I heard of a young woman named Odessa who she took in and cared for her and gave her guidance after her family had cut her off because she had two kids before she was married. Then there was Patricia, who had a young son she was trying her best to raise on her own; she worked two jobs to make ends meet, so you can only imagine she needs help raising her son. My grandmother took her son in like he was her own grandchild; she often watched him until the wee hours of the morning, free of charge, and she helped Patricia with food if she needed it.

Granny was what I call an Urban Angel, who tried to look out for those less fortunate souls in the hood. When I think of other Urban Angels, I think of a loving and proud woman I had the pleasure of knowing, a woman I affectionately called Aunt Barbara. She wasn't related to me in blood, but our families were so close; she was just like my blood relative. She lived on Hawkins Street in the

Ironbound area of Newark with her husband, Richard, and her son, Richard Jr., and her daughter, Pamela. Those who are familiar with Newark think of the Ironbound section as one of the better areas of Newark, and it is, except for a couple of notorious housing projects. One of those projects is the Hawkins Street Projects. Hawkins Street, like most low-income housing areas, was filled with poverty and plenty of criminal activity. Aunt Barbara always kept her head up, kept her kids in check, and even raised four other foster kids with the help of her loving husband. All together, this loving Urban Angel raised one son (he is a retired naval officer), a biological daughter (she's a teacher), and two adopted sons, who have good jobs and are now married with families. She did have two adopted sons who fell victim to the streets (one was killed unfortunately and one who's currently serving time in prison), but Lord knows she tried. My aunt Barbara passed several years ago; the night we heard of her passing, it rained cats and dogs the rest of that evening. It seems ironic; I like to say on that night, the clouds were crying at the passing of a good model of kindness and loving grace.

In my old building, Brick Towers (man oh man, no matter where I go or what I do, I eventually comes back to Brick Towers), there was another Urban Angel who lived on the sixth floor. Jeanette had three sons and two daughters of her own, and when her kids were of age and out on their own, she took in three foster kids and raised them until they were grown as well. Jeanette often looked out for me and other kids in our hood; as we were growing up, she was there to put us in check if we needed it, and she was there to offer us a comforting hand if we needed it.

These are just examples of Urban Angels, and I want to bring their stories to the entire nation so that these unwavering, unselfish angels can get some of the acclaim and recognition they deserve. In Islam, paradise is given to those who take in foster kids. God bless our Urban Angels through this nation and the world, and please know, whether people recognize your efforts or not, the gates of heaven await you.

17-May-2014

It's March 21, 2019. What a beautiful day outside; it's a picture-perfect day for the first day of spring. I wake up with my beautiful wife lying next to me. After I make my morning prayers, I go check on Amir; he is now five years old and growing taller, stronger, smarter, and more handsome every day. Then I go check on my mother in the guest room; all praise is due to Allah for giving her good health to still be here with me. I can't thank him enough. After I make sure everyone is all right, I lay back down with my wife. I look at the clock and see that it's only 7:30 and it's Saturday, so why not? Me and the wife are off, and our son is off from school, so it's a nice day to sleep in late.

As I lay back down, I can't help but start thinking about my life and how blessed I am to be where I am, considering where I came from. I am humbled by the mercy God has shown me, and of course I'm grateful. No matter how humbled I get, there's still a fire in me that wants to go further and see just how far life can take me. While I'm here on earth, I wanna live this life and reach the pinnacle of whatever success is intended for me. That's just my nature; I'm always striving for more. I want more, and by the grace of God, I won't stop until I get more. But I'm gonna do it the right way; of course, I don't wanna hurt anyone or fuck anybody over to get what I need. I believe this is one of the keys to longevity. Because after all, if you wake up every day with nothing to look forward to and you have no goals, then what's your motivation to keep living?

Stagnant water is dead and lifeless; it's good to be motivated and keep it moving. I have been working for CNN for three years now, and I have loved every minute of it. The salary is very good, and along with my police pension, I'm doing well. I have always loved writing, but I'm ready to take my writing to the next level. I want to be an author. It would seem almost natural; I spent twenty-five years of my life writing police reports for perfect strangers, and I now write articles for a news media giant, so why not do some writing for myself? It's time for me to blow myself up. I always said I want to know what it feels like to be a millionaire before I leave this earth. My pension is good, and my new career pays me decent, but I'm never gonna be a millionaire working for somebody else. I heard slow and steady wins the race; maybe so, but you gotta be in it to win it. So I'm gonna go for it. I have no intentions on quitting my day job, but I will set aside a couple of hours every day for myself to concentrate on writing my book; with the help of God, I'll have the book finished within six months. I do love my job and adore the atmosphere where I work; in fact, I love it a little too much, if you know what I mean.

A few years ago, I almost got myself into trouble with Elaina (remember her? That sexy, sensual Latina who looked in incredible in her heels). Well, in the CNN building and in the surrounding area, there are hundreds of Elainas around me all day in different shades, and that takes a toll on a brother. I'm trying to be faithful. I don't by any stretch of the imagination wanna be in the situation I was a few years back. It's just as a man, my mind says one thing, and that bad boy between my legs says something else (I swear, sometimes he has a mind of his own).

Some might say it's not hard keep your joint in your pants, and they would be right. But that's easier said than done in this environment; when I was younger and didn't have a girl, I couldn't get a girl. It's usually like that with women; now, I have a beautiful wife (one of the worst mistakes I made was bringing my wife to a holiday party at CNN; once the ladies saw her, they started pushing up. Now I gotta fight those hoes off. Their logic is crazy, and if a brother is not careful, you can get caught up).

So that's another motivator toward becoming financially independent. Over the past few years, I've been pretty good (not great but pretty good) at keeping my joint to myself. I must admit I've had a couple of slip-ups. I had to hit up Elaina a couple more times; I know, I'm a dog to some extent, but any man who would get a look at her would know where I'm coming from.

And then there was Evette, who worked in accounts payable; my nickname for her was simply Body. Lord knows, she had a body that could stop traffic. After those two, I was good for about a year and a half. I was real good until I met Katherine, a white girl with long dark hair, light blue eyes, and body that a sister would envy. Don't speak too harshly of me; I only screwed her twice. I could have gotten more, and believe me, I wanted to, but I couldn't keep doing that to my babe. After all, I'm a married man.

My first book will be a love story of a young man and woman who both grow in poverty and the hardships of the urban struggles and become honor students and go to college at Grambling University, where they meet and eventually get married. They have great success in their careers; he's an engineer and she is a lawyer. I have other stories in mind, like an urban horror story and a book on the strained relationship between police departments and the citizens in urban communities (you know I had to throw in a book about the police).

18-May-2014

I OFTEN GO BACK TO MY OLD NEIGHBORHOOD, perhaps just to remember some of the old times (the good ones, that is). I also know that the Central Ward was a place where I had many bad moments, moments that I can proudly say would have broken a lesser man. At this point in my life, I'm proud to say I came from this inner city hell and became the man that I am today. One of the main reasons I come here is to remind myself that I never want to come back to this again. This is the main reason why I work so hard and will continue to strive so hard for success. I've been here, done this, and don't ever want to return to it. When I return to the old hood, I see so much has changed over the years, but just the scenery. The inner problems have stayed the same; the projects have been replaced with townhouses, but the drug problems and the crime rate are still the same. Poverty hasn't changed; it is still epidemic. I still see young girls who are babies themselves having babies. It only shows that putting a pretty bandage on a wound won't always cure the wound. Allah says in the Holy Koran that he won't change the condition of a people until they change the condition of their heart. As I ride from MLK Blvd. to Muhammad Ali Avenue over to Irving Turner Blvd., I think to myself, *Damn, it's almost like time has stood still in this hood.*

Of course, certain things look different, but I'm speaking about the condition of the people, the mentality of the people. It saddens me because even though I had more than my share of nightmares growing up here, this will always be home. I've always had this love-hate relationship with the Central, even when I was a cop. Ironically, this is the same relationship I had with my father. As much as I hated him and his bullshit, I couldn't help but love him because, after all, he was my father.

After I finished my visit of the old hood, on my way home, I had an inspiration for a future book, a motivational book of awareness for those who live in the urban inner cities. Naturally, I want all people from all walks of life to read my books; my books are for all people. I think those people who live in the urban inner cities can benefit a little more from that book when it's written. But first things first: I have to finish the first book and go from there. I started on the book a few weeks ago, and it's going well so far. It's not always easy getting that free time where I can get away and take time to write. I have a lot going on with work, then I have to get my workout in, then there's the wife. I also have to take care of Momma, and of course I make as much time as I can to spend with my little man, Amir. I determined to have a great relationship with my son; this is not gonna be anything like my relationship with my father.

I take my time with this book, writing a little here and there when I get a chance to. I don't put too much pressure on myself. I've noticed for me when I take my time with things, they usually work out better for me.

So six months went by, and I finished. I really believed in this book, so after work, I took it to this publishing company down the street from my job. I spoke to them previously about the book, so they were expecting me; it also helps that they know I'm a writer for CNN. Often publishing companies are a little leery about working with a new writer, so it helps to have a foot in the door. After leaving the publishing company, I got on the train and headed home. I shared the news with my wife and family, and that evening, I took everyone out for a celebration dinner. Now that the work has been put in, we'll just wait and see the results. I know I have to be patient; the whole process takes a little time. They have to copyedit it and put it out there for the readers. So I'm gonna keep doing my usual in the meantime and wait for the good news. Positive thinking is a motherfucker, and that's the way I'm gonna think; no time for negativity in my world.

I have started on my next book; I just changed the order in which I'm going to write the books. I decided to make the next book about awareness in urban hoods. The horror story can wait; after all, there are plenty of people in the inner cities who live a horror story every day. Hopefully, the book on awareness can help in some way; even if it's just in a very small way, it could help make some of my brothers and sister reach higher and never give in.

19-May-2014

Four months after I finished my book, I started to get my royalties. I'm getting some pretty good money, some damn good money; the book is going very well. My publisher tells me that they think this book is really gonna take off; man, am I excited. At last a chance to come off and make it big. My wife was ecstatic when I told her the news; my mom told me that she has been proud of me for so long now, considering how I got my life together and became an officer and a journalist, but she told me she was at a loss for words; never in her wildest dreams did she expect for me to go this far in life.

Her words meant so much to me; coming from where I came from, you're considered very fortunate if you grow up, manage to get a halfway good job, and make it to forty without dying, going to jail, or getting killed. So what if a brother finishes a good career, starts another good career, and then has the potential to really blow up and possibly get into that exclusive millionaires' club? But I'm not going to get ahead of myself. I'm not there yet, so I still have a ways to go, and I'm gonna keep doing my usual: go to work and keep working hard and taking care of the family. People at work are starting to congratulate me on the book; word got out quickly in the building about my book, which is good thing, especially if everyone in the building goes out and buys a copy.

A few more months went by, and I'm almost finished with my second book. This is the one I really wanna push because this is the one I think can help make a difference in some lives, which is important to me because just like everyone else, I wanna achieve my success in this world, but I feel when you have been blessed by the very best (almighty God) to achieve good fortune, you have the responsibility to give back to your community, to society as a whole. When I was younger, I tried to mentally distance myself from my neighborhood. I tried to reject where I came from; I had animosity and anger because of the way I grew up, but as I grew older and wiser, I realized Newark, the Central Ward, Brick Towers, the projects: All of this is gonna be a part of me forever, and there's no way around it, so now I just focus on the valuable lessons that I learned from growing up there. I use those lessons wherever I encounter a struggle or a hardship in life.

One evening as I was sitting home, watching a movie with my family, I got a call from my publisher, and he said that my book just made the best-sellers list. Upon hearing the news, I almost fainted, I was so excited. I quickly got myself together. I couldn't afford to get sick now that I'm about to starting this money. I gotta stick around to spend some of it. I break the news to the family, and we had a celebration.

The next day, I still went to work; a brother is not going to change. I'm gonna keep this job; the only difference being once the big money from the book comes in, I might just try to see if I can stay on with the company as a freelance writer instead of an everyday employee. Just like before, word of my success leaked out quickly. If I thought women were coming at me before, now with this new-found success, they were on me like flies on shit. That's not a good thing for me; I still have that little sickness when it comes to the ladies. I've been good for a while now, and I wanna stay good. That's another reason why I try to stay busy; this way, there are as few distractions as possible. I have even taken to eating my lunch at my desk so I don't have to look at all of that eye candy in the area. It seems as though having success is in fact starting to make me wiser because now I have a great deal to lose, and the last thing I need to do is get someone else pregnant. Also, who needs to take the risk of catching some disease? We all know that everything that looks good ain't good.

At this moment in life, I'm in a great place so I'm taking it slow and easy. Now that the money is coming in, it's time for me to make certain moves. I purchased a couple of properties, two in Newark and three in Irvington. You can never go wrong with real estate. I want a steady money flow coming in that is also a secure investment. I then took care of people in my family who always stood by me, no matter the situation.

From there, it was now time to do what I talked about before (and honestly speaking, something I've always tried to do): give back to my community. I went into partnership with George Mercer, an old friend of mine from grammar school who played eight years in the NFL. We started a nonprofit house for orphaned kids and kids who have been the victim of sex abuse. I took a leave of absence from CNN to manage the business while it we got it started. I also used this time to finish my second book. This is the one I can't wait to get out there. Like I said before, now it's time to give back. I feel so blessed with the good fortune God has given me, so now I feel obligated to give back to those less fortunate and to use my resources to possibly help them improve their situation.

20-May-2014

I'M DETERMINED NOT TO LET SUCCESS AND money change me. I gonna stay the same person that I have always been. I've never been the type to keep a large entourage of people around me. I never liked crowds like that. Even when the publishers scheduled a book signing for me, I couldn't wait until it was over. All of the attention made me feel uncomfortable, but I understand it's all part of the process, so I go along with it. Inside, however, I wish all I had to do was just sit back and collect the money (lol). I like being low key; it's just hard being low key when you have certain positions, like when I was a cop, a lot of times I just couldn't be low key. I assume the same things could apply when you have money; it's been my experience in this life that most people in general are naturally nosy by nature, so somebody is gonna notice you.

I remember at some roll calls, before I would go out on patrol, some cops would be so nosy; they would immediately notice if you had on a new pair of shoes or a new uniform shirt. I know that will be the price that comes with money and success; the haters will be there, and sometimes people you have known for years will be jealous of your good fortune. I'm not gonna worry about that; the way I look at is like this: I know I'm not the type of person who thinks I'm better than anybody. I stay down to earth and grounded, and whenever I can, I try to look out for people, so anyone who has a beef with me for being blessed is a real insignificant ass hole not even worth conversation. Now that I'm doing well with the first book, I'm trying to focus my attention on the new book; now with the help of God, if the second one goes well, I would like to write a few plays and possibly get a publishing company of my own in the future. Then again, I don't wanna jump the gun. I'll just stick with my same routine, one thing at a time. The first book is done and doing well; my side ventures are up and running well, thanks to some help from some close friends I have confidence in. My lifelong friend Marcus has a degree in business management; he just retired from Ford Motor Co. and is managing my nonprofit business, along with George Mercer. My cousin Andrea is a property manager in real estate, so she manages my properties for me. Now that my side ventures are doing fine, it's time to get back to work. I almost feel like a celebrity by the way everyone is treating me at work. Even some members of the executive board invited me upstairs to congratulate me on my book. They talked about throwing me a little gathering in the lunch room to celebrate. At first, I didn't want to do it because like I said, I'm a low key kind of guy. After I thought about it, I decided to go through with it; you know, if somebody is gonna do something for you free of charge, with no strings attached, why not?

After the party, I was ready to get back to work as usual, so the next day, I came in like nothing had ever happened. In my mind, I was no celebrity, and I came to work as though it was my first day and I was a hungry young reporter, starving for an opportunity. One of the many lessons I have learned in life is to keep working just as hard when you get a few dollars as you did when you were broke because when you stay hungry, that helps keep you from ever going broke. You must keep that hunger. Remember, you always need something to strive for.

So once I got back to work, the network gave me exactly what I needed: a detailed assignment that would challenge not only my writing skills but also my investigative skills. This assignment called for me to travel to Liberia in West Africa. The story is about young women who are being held captive as modern-day slaves and used in prostitution rings. For this assignment, I will need a good crew with me, so I asked for my old friend Elaina. I know, why would I put myself in another situation with her, but this is business, and she is very good at her job.

I also need my man Frank, who very professional and a very hard worker. This is a story that is near and dear to my heart because

I hate hearing stories of women being abused, and the ones who are supposed to be responsible for this abuse are radical Islamic militants. As a Muslim, I'm taking this story very seriously because the world needs to know that Islam as a religion has never condoned atrocities like this. This conduct goes totally against Al Islam.

21-May-2014

FROM THE MOMENT MY TEAM AND I got on the plane and all the way through the ten-hour flight, my adrenaline was pumping. This assignment could make me or break me in this field; this story could win me a Pulitzer Prize. But it would be even more satisfying to me if by getting this story out there to the world, it would help to liberate these young women and help get them home safely to their families. That would be much more gratifying to me than any prize. These young women needed help, and I hoped my article would help the rest of the world pay attention and put their resources together to assist them. I find it so disturbing that in the modern world, we still have this kind of treatment of women going on; this shit seems so medieval. It does exist, however, so now it's time to confront the problem.

Upon arrival in Liberia, we were met by some members of the country's security forces. That's one thing about working for a media giant; on assignments where there is a definite threat of danger, the company will make your safety a top priority. We stayed in the Royal Grand Hotel in the heart of the business district of Monrovia, the capital of Liberia. The hotel was luxurious, with all the modern appliances you would expect in a five-star hotel. The rooms were spacious, and the room service was the best I've ever experienced.

I made sure not to get too comfortable with the environment; I had to keep my focus, keep my edge, so to speak. I was here to get this story out so that enough of the world would stand up and make some noise and do something about these injustices. The media has a lot of power throughout the world; the media may arguably be the most powerful influencing tool on this planet. So if used correctly, this story will save some lives. In fact, maybe I'm reaching a little too far, but perhaps this story can get the ball rolling toward permanently ending practices like this.

A very wise man once stated that you can tell the condition of a people by the condition of the women in that nation. That is why in my story, I will make a plea to the entire world, but especially the men of the African continent and in particular the Muslim men, to take a stand against this radical group. They not only disgrace this great continent, they disgrace the beautiful religion of Al Islam. A few years ago, right after the scare that I had with Elaina, you couldn't have gotten me to stay in a luxury hotel with her in the very next room. Hell no, not after what happened. Believe me, she is still fine as wine, and I still fight my demons regularly. It's just that on this trip, there was no room for weakness. I was on a mission from God; lives need saving. Much work needs to be done. I was as focused as I've ever been in my life. While we're working, my crew and I made time for rest, and we had some great conversations. I get a sense, however, that everyone here knows the importance of this story and what the stakes are, so we are all focused to the max.

We were able to gather a great deal of information; when we spoke to some of the families who had lost daughters, sisters, cousins, nieces, and so on, I left some of the homes with tears in my eyes. After speaking to them, I went around to different mosques in the area and spoke to the different leaders of the more moderate Muslim communities in Liberia. I was very pleased with the results of our meetings; the men of these communities told me that they were not only outraged by the actions of these so-called Islamic militants, they made a vow to get out and help the Liberian police and security forces in their effort to locate and bring these girls home safely, doing everything they can to help end this sickening trend. Once we finished gathering information for the story, we were ready to head back to the States and make some noise.

Once my feet hit US soil, the first stop I made was back to the office. I went there to get the story started. I called Jennifer, who is (and always has been) my rock, my foundation, and told her what I was gonna do. She was understanding, as always. My team and I stayed up the rest of the night working on that story; we didn't finish until eight o'clock in the morning. We were all so hyped up that we didn't notice the time. Once we finished it, we looked it over and turned it in to the editors for review. I think I was more excited about this story than my own books. I felt like I had a mission with this assignment.

22-May-2014

ONCE THE STORY WAS RELEASED TO THE public, I was very pleased; there were many cries from all over the world for justice for these young women. Stories came from several other media outlets all over the world. The story didn't get me a Pulitzer award, but it did get me nominated for a Mike Berger Award for a thought-provoking human interest story. I didn't win the award, but you know, I was cool with that; just being nominated for such a prestigious award was a great honor for me. Things were going so well for me in life that I was almost afraid. I'm not used to having such good fortune and I was starting to think, *Oh my God, there has to be some major catastrophe around the corner.* Then it came to me: stop thinking negative; you know better than that. Enjoy the good that's here now. Lord knows I've had my share of BS in life, so maybe things are just balancing their way out. Don't wait for misfortune; let it have to find me, so for now, I'm gonna ride this good wave until goes flat.

The wave continued too; a few days after the award ceremony, I was advised by my publisher that my second book was doing well in the stores, so I was on my way. I took my family on a well-deserved vacation to the Bahamas, deluxe accommodations with everything included. My wife really deserved that and so much more for standing behind me the way she did and being so understanding of all of the long hours I have put in at work over the last few years. She is a real soldier for the cause.

On this trip, I gave her a little token of my appreciation. I bought a 24-carat diamond, and little did she know, when we got back home, I had a new Mercedes 500 Class waiting for her. She deserves it and more for dealing with my black ass. I would have gotten Mom one too, but she doesn't drive, so I got her a diamond necklace.

We enjoyed the Bahamas, and the great thing about it was now that I had the financial security I've been seeking my whole life, we could take trips like this more often. Once we got home, I had a little thinking to do. I had two best-selling books out, I had properties, a business, and a great job, so what is my complaint? Absolutely nothing. I just can't handle all of these endeavors at once. It seems like I might have reached a little too high on this one; even a motivated soldier like me can't handle all this work (lol). So after careful consideration, I decided to keep everything; you can never have enough security in this life. What I'm gonna do is follow my initial thought and work for CNN as a freelance writer; that will give me more freedom to concentrate on my businesses. I have trusted people helping me with the business and my properties, and I have my wife as my business partner. She is thorough as hell, so I'm not worried about nobody getting over on us. I'm good.

I can't and won't give up CNN totally; not just because it pays well, but the media power is a hard thing to give up. The pen is much mightier than the sword. Now that I have my priorities in order, it's time to sit back and enjoy the fruits of my labor with all of my loved ones. My life has been some adventure; it reminds me of a rollercoaster ride, with all of the highs and the lows. Then maybe when I think about it, that's pretty much everybody's life. Of course, some people may have it a bit easier than others, but I'm pretty sure we all have a story to tell. In the beginning, I thought my story was bound to have a bad ending. It just goes to show you can't give up; just because things don't start off well, you can never tell what the future holds. Strong faith and hard work never go unrewarded. I once thought I was born in hell on earth. If that was the case, I'm here to say that you can escape that hell on earth, with God's help and perseverance. Challenges make you stronger; only the strong will survive in this world. The greatest strength comes from inside the mind and soul. Life will take many twists and turns; some for the better, some for the worst. So in hard times, you must hang on, be strong, and fight hard for your right to success and happiness.

23-May-2014

M*I VIDA LOCA* MEANS "MY CRAZY LIFE" in Spanish. My life has been crazy for sure; I feel like I've seen it all, but I haven't. You learn something new every day, see something different every minute, hear something you never heard before every second. This is just life at its best and at its worst; all I can do is just keep living. Just when I was ready to give up on life, God the almighty showed me that life was not ready to give up on me. Life is so precious; cherish your existence and stay focused. Look at where I came from and where I'm at. So many times, I just wanted to curl up under a rock and die. When I was young and living in Brick Towers, it felt like I was in giant casket; in fact, being surrounded by nothing but projects, the whole ward used to feel like a brick casket. But I hung in there. Imagine if I had given up. I try to live by the motto "No retreat, no surrender." There is only one way to be a winner: You must play the game. The best advice I can give anyone is this: Wake up every day that you are blessed to wake up, with one thing on your mind: I'm gonna win in this game called life. I'm gonna win if it kills me. I am Hakim Jones, and this was my story, from trials to tragedy to triumph.

25-May-2014

The Thin Blue Line

PRIOR TO BECOMING A COP, I USED to hear about that blue wall amongst the police fraternity; you know, it was said how cops stick together, they never rat each other out, they never go against another cop, no matter what the circumstances are. Even if a cop is dead wrong on something, you as a brother officer correct him in private, not in public, because when it's all said and done, as cops, we are all we have out there. I can tell you from first-hand experience, once you become a cop, it is almost like now it's you against the world. I can also tell from experience that the so-called blue wall, at least by the time I was ready to leave the job, had a big break in it. I'm not gonna lie; after twenty-five years on the streets of Brick City, I was more than ready to call it a career, but I for damn sure didn't have any inclination to stay on this job after seeing how officers no longer had the same sense of loyalty and respect for each other like they used to.

When I first started on this job, when a cop came into contact when another cop, whether the cop worked at his precinct or for another department, it didn't matter: cops took care of cops. You never crossed that blue line. Those cops who did cross the line were quickly classed as outcast; no one wanted anything to do with them. They were labeled a scumbag, traitor, piece of shit, and many other names of choice. This police shit was supposed to be a fraternity like no other; we were supposed to be one giant brotherhood, fighting for the same cause of upholding the law. As officers, we would often joke that the police were the biggest gang in the world; even street gangs looked at us like that, and you could see why by the way we stuck together and all had one color in common: blue.

As my career was ending, even the gangsters and criminals on the street could sense that the police were just not the same cohesive unit they once were; I guess you could say we followed the same trend that most gangs do: We began to split up into groups, fractions, and sects. I could tell by the way they acted toward us; the respect that they would show a cop back when I first started this job was a hell of a lot different than it was at the end of my career. It was all because they could see a division amongst the ranks. Once your house is divided, that's usually a prelude to falling apart. The problem is that the way things are these days, everyone has their own separate agendas; that sense of loyalty and brotherhood is gone. Now let me again make it perfectly clear: I am not an advocate of standing behind someone who is doing wrong, whether he wears a badge and gun or not. I am an advocate of fighting to the end with fellow officers if they are standing up for what is supposed to be the same cause all of us are supposed to be standing up for: the cause of justice.

Uniformity is key to keeping any organization functioning well. From the first day I started the academy, I was told that we are all blue, no matter what, regardless of your race, religion, or gender. After a while, however, you start to see that things are still divided into clans and certain groups, and if you're not part of a particular group, while they won't necessarily go out of their way to hurt you or cause you any problems, the same rules that apply to those who are part of the "in crowd" will most certainly not apply to those officers who just stay to themselves.

To put it in laymen's terms, being a loner is not at all beneficial to you in this field; for that matter, just like in everyday life, being a loner in today's world does not serve you well, in no way, shape, or form. On this job, rules that should apply to everyone don't apply to the privileged ones. Any disciplinary trials can be a farce; some cops may call me a turncoat for saying this, but I'm all in favor of a civilian review board. Let's face it: I don't think policing will ever be like it once was; like most trends, when change comes, it rarely if ever goes back to the way it was, and for me that's fine. As I've said before, life should be about progress; you can't make progress going backward. You must move forward and adapt to what's around and work with the cards that you've been dealt.

With a civilian review board that is carefully selected, with impartial members with no ties to anyone, maybe everyone can have a fair and level playing field to play on, not just the selected few. Hypocrisy is something I have always hated. I'm not claiming to be perfect (never have, never will), but I can't with a clear conscience try to enforce something on someone else when I'm guilty of doing the same thing. Who's knows, maybe I'm the one who's crazy, but I don't believe in the philosophy "Do as I say, not as I do."

Most people I have found, especially some cops, feel as though the rules only apply when they are beneficial to them; when it's not, they just skip over that rule. I say that's a bunch of crap. In the Koran, Allah tells us that the hypocrites will be fuel for the hell fire, and I see why. I often found my father to be very hypocritical. I don't know, maybe he is the underlying reason for my passionate stance against those who practice flagrant hypocrisy, but this who I am, take it or leave it. I can't see wrong and not at least speak about it. Today in this game, there is no honor among thieves, so to speak. The blue line is a thing of the past.

26-May-2014

There is no substitute for good planning. I was told by someone very wise and intelligent that a man without a plan is not a man; of course, this was probably a quote he got from some philosopher I'm unaware of, but this statement is so true, nonetheless. This is often one of the biggest elements missing from a lot of us who grow up in the urban inner cities. I'm just gonna keep it real and say what I mean. This missing link is often missing from most black kids growing up in the inner cities. In any aspect of life, having a plan is essential to being successful in this world, unless you are fortunate to be born into a rich family (and even then it's good to have some type of plan to keep the money flow coming in so that you won't go broke). In life, anything can be had at any moment, of course, but I've never been a big believer in luck. The definition of luck is usually described as when preparation and opportunity meet. Growing up the way I did, I had no real guidance toward a career or career goals. Even though I went to a vocational school, they never helped me as far as finding a job when I left there, and the administration damn sure didn't help a brother toward getting in any trade unions.

Then again, in cases like this with these unions and union jobs, the ugly head of racism exists and is often just as prevalent as it was in the 1940s. Racism will always exist, but like most obstacles in life, it's just one more thing that you have to get around and keep moving forward in spite of. I have often used it as one of my motivational tools when trying to move forward toward success. So with all of that being said, this is all the more reason why it's vital to have a good plan of action when moving forward in life. As I have studied young men of other races and cultures, I have seen that most of them start planning for their futures at much younger ages, and when they finish high school, they start implementing their plan. Whether it's going to college, getting started on their own business, going to the military, getting into a trade union, taking a civil service job, or whatever, they get started at a younger age than most African American males.

You can't blame the system or even society for this; you may ask why I say this after I've stated how racism is still so prevalent in this world. My reason is because even with race being a factor, when you have a strong family foundation that supports each other toward improving their lives and moving forward as a whole, even the ugly head of racism will have great difficulty trying to hold a person back. All of this again goes back to having a plan. In my time on this earth, I have seen men of other cultures make certain sacrifices so that future generations of their kind will have it better than they did, and they further instill that way of thinking into their kids, who in turn teach this to their kids and so on.

In essence, this way of thinking is a plan of strategy, which can have such a profound effect on life if you don't have one. Even during my college years, of course, my immediate goal was to finish, but I still wasn't too sure about my long-range goal. Initially, my major wasn't criminal justice; it was computer programming. It turned out that this course of study was a little too tedious for me, and I later switched to criminal justice. After the switch, I still had no I idea that I would become a cop. It wasn't until after I became a cop that my life really found some direction in life. Like most young men who grow up in a situation similar to mine, I just survived day to day, hoping that a break would come along.

Yes, I myself was guilty of not making plans. In Islam, there is a belief that whatever happens to you in life was meant to happen to you, and whatever passes you by was meant to pass you by. I'm a firm believer in this, so what's done is done. There's nothing I can do about the past, but there's a whole hell of a lot I can try to do for my future, God willing. One thing I do, always and for the rest of my life, is make plans, even if it's just plans for the weekend. I know that God is the best of planners, no doubt, but as individuals, we can't just sit back and hope for the best without putting our best foot forward in an effort to make things happen. To be effective at accomplishing your goals requires much careful planning.